The Open Door

Also From Laurelin Paige

Slay Series
Slay One: Rivalry
Slay Two: Ruin
Slay Three: Revenge – coming soon
Slay Four: Rising – coming soon

The Fixed Series
Fixed on You
Found in You
Forever with You
Hudson
Falling Under You: A Fixed Trilogy Novella (1001 Dark Nights)
Chandler
Dirty, Filthy Fix: A Fixed Trilogy Novella (1001 Dark Nights)
Fixed Forever

Dirty Universe
Dirty Filthy Rich Boys
Dirty Filthy Rich Men
Dirty Filthy Rich Love
Dirty, Sexy Player
Dirty Sexy Games
Sweet Liar
Sweet Fate

Found Duet
Free Me
Find Me

First and Last
First Touch
Last Kiss

Hollywood Heat
Sex Symbol

Star Struck
One More Time
Close

The Open Door
A Found Duet Novella

By Laurelin Paige

1001 Dark Nights

EVIL EYE
CONCEPTS

The Open Door
A Found Duet Novella
By Laurelin Paige

1001 Dark Nights
Copyright 2019 Laurelin Paige
ISBN: 978-1-948050-97-5

Foreword: Copyright 2014 M. J. Rose
Published by Evil Eye Concepts, Incorporated

Dedication

Dedicated to all those kinky women who are still madly in love after being married for more than a minute.

Sign up for the 1001 Dark Nights Newsletter
and be entered to win a Tiffany Key necklace.

There's a contest every month!

Go to www.1001DarkNights.com to subscribe.

**As a bonus, all subscribers can download
FIVE FREE exclusive books!**

One Thousand and One Dark Nights

Once upon a time, in the future…

I was a student fascinated with stories and learning.
I studied philosophy, poetry, history, the occult, and
the art and science of love and magic. I had a vast
library at my father's home and collected thousands
of volumes of fantastic tales.

I learned all about ancient races and bygone
times. About myths and legends and dreams of all
people through the millennium. And the more I read
the stronger my imagination grew until I discovered
that I was able to travel into the stories… to actually
become part of them.

I wish I could say that I listened to my teacher
and respected my gift, as I ought to have. If I had, I
would not be telling you this tale now.
But I was foolhardy and confused, showing off
with bravery.

One afternoon, curious about the myth of the
Arabian Nights, I traveled back to ancient Persia to
see for myself if it was true that every day Shahryar
(Persian: شهریار, "king") married a new virgin, and then
sent yesterday's wife to be beheaded. It was written
and I had read, that by the time he met Scheherazade,
the vizier's daughter, he'd killed one thousand
women.

Something went wrong with my efforts. I arrived in the midst of the story and somehow exchanged places with Scheherazade — a phenomena that had never occurred before and that still to this day, I cannot explain.

Now I am trapped in that ancient past. I have taken on Scheherazade's life and the only way I can protect myself and stay alive is to do what she did to protect herself and stay alive.

Every night the King calls for me and listens as I spin tales. And when the evening ends and dawn breaks, I stop at a point that leaves him breathless and yearning for more. And so the King spares my life for one more day, so that he might hear the rest of my dark tale.

As soon as I finish a story... I begin a new one... like the one that you, dear reader, have before you now.

Chapter One

Interested?

The subject line in the email my husband had forwarded was intriguing, to say the least. When the notification popped up on my phone, I felt the pull to read it right away.

But Braden needed a diaper change, Jake was kicking at the door of his bedroom where he was currently in time out, and I'd just discovered Theo had found a black marker. The kid desperately needed a bath and my hallway now needed a new paint job.

I pocketed my phone, balanced the baby on my hip, and let out a slow breath while I counted to ten before ushering Theo to the nursery with me.

Motherhood wasn't always this hectic, I reminded myself. Today was only chaotic because JC was out of town working on one of his investment projects, and the nanny didn't work on Sundays. While both my husband and I worked full time, we were really hands-on with our parenting. Sundays and Mondays were our weekends. Neither of us worked on these days, for the most part, and we only brought the nanny in when absolutely necessary. When JC had told me on Saturday that he needed to extend his trip in Chicago for another day, I'd considered calling Ruth to help out but decided against it. I could handle three boys under six on my own for a little while, couldn't I?

The answer was yes. But it definitely took every last drop of my energy. Even running a summer Friday night shift at The Sky Launch, the night club I co-managed, was easier than this.

"It's worth it," I told Braden as I laid him down on the changing table. I even meant it.

Mostly.

It was another two hours before I had the kids clean, fed, and settled enough to look at my phone. I shifted a sleeping Braden off my breast and into a position where I had a hand to use. Then I went to my notifications and opened the email JC had sent earlier.

Besides the tantalizing subject line, all that was inside the message was a website link along with a username and password. I clicked on the link and awkwardly entered the information he'd provided with my free hand—my non-dominant hand, hence the awkward.

I blinked at the bold red headline that popped up: **Welcome to The Open Door**.

My breath hitched when I recognized what exactly The Open Door was. I'd heard of it before, it came up from time to time in social situations, especially ones that included the richest of the rich and the cream of the crop of socialites. Honestly, I'd thought the thing was a hoax, a lavish fantasy that sprung from the heads of bored housewives and restless entrepreneurs. A super hush-hush, organized, weekly sex party hosted by the elite of New York City? Total fairytale. Who wouldn't want to believe that existed?

But here seemed to be proof that it wasn't just an elaborate rumor.

A thrill ran down my spine, and my pulse sped up. This was sensational. Scandalous, even. With this email, I'd become privy to a secret society. Even if we never did anything with that information—because, seriously, why would we—how could it not be exciting?

But then I read through the rest of the information on my screen, a list of dates and locations as well as terms and instructions, and realized that this wasn't just a cool bit of gossip that my husband had stumbled upon. It was an invitation. An invitation that JC had accepted when he set up an account. And based on what I was reading about the benefits of membership, the fees to join had been outrageous.

Sure, we could afford it. JC was born of means and his passion for investing in promising start-up companies had paid off well. We weren't big spenders, generally—our tastes and needs were more simple than extravagant—but the money was there when and if we wanted it. So it wasn't the cost that was giving me anxiety.

It was the simple fact that my husband, the man who had seemingly been happy with what happened in our bedroom for the last eight years, had signed us both up for a sex club.

A sex club!

A place for swingers and orgies and kink.

I wasn't a prude—not since I'd met JC, anyway—but I was a one-man kind of woman. And, while we sometimes used butt plugs and vibrators and handcuffs in the privacy of our own love nest, I'd never needed or wanted anything more extreme.

When did *JC* start wanting it? And why hadn't he ever said anything to me? Was he totally bored with me? Had breastfeeding and a C-section and not enough time in the gym destroyed my body? Was I no longer desirable?

Was I not enough?

After all I gave to the man, I better be e-fucking-nough. I worked hard, mothered his kids, put dinners on the table, put out on a very regular basis. Maybe not as regularly as when we'd been childless, but come on. What did he expect? We had three fucking kids. I barely had time to brush my teeth, let alone be sexy. He was lucky I ever had the energy to spread my legs. I was as good as reality gets.

Apparently not so good that he didn't think we required outside intervention.

I didn't know whether to be hurt or pissed. Frankly, I was both.

But the baby was stirring and Theo was screaming because Jake, who was about to have another time out, had just pushed him off the ladder of his Little Tikes slide.

Motherhood didn't leave a lot of time to be hurt and pissed at husbands. At least not while the children were still awake.

Fine. I could shelve the feelings for the moment. But just wait until JC was home and the kids were in bed. I was confident I could spare enough time then to be as hurt and pissed as I wanted to be.

Chapter Two

"The baby's got his butt sticking straight up in the air," JC said, chuckling, as he came into the bedroom.

He'd arrived home only fifteen minutes before, long after the boys had gone down for the night. I'd given him a quick recap of his time away, mostly highlighting events with the kids, then, as to be expected, he'd wanted to sneak in and check on them all before giving his attention to me.

He went to his side of the bed, took his watch off and set it on his nightstand. "Theo's still sucking his thumb in his sleep. Should we be worried about that?"

I'd already dressed for bed, donning one of JC's T-shirts, and was now leaning against the headboard with my laptop. With my boss out on her own maternity leave, I had an extra load at the nightclub, and I'd found working from bed had become an unfortunate nightly ritual.

I looked up from the screen and blinked, trying to focus on what my husband had just asked. "Dr. Agarwal said she wasn't concerned as long it was restricted to naps and bedtime. Was Jacob asleep in his bed? Yesterday, he was curled up on the floor when I went in to check on him."

"That kid." His blue eyes glazed with love for his boys as he toed off his shoes. He'd lost his suit jacket somewhere else in the house. I made a mental note to find it in the morning and make sure it made it to his closet. "Yeah. He was in his bed. He was tangled in his covers so I straightened them out and tucked him in."

JC pulled his belt from the loops of his pants and dropped it to the floor before crawling across the mattress in my direction.

"Your suit is going to get wrinkled," I warned, more a wifely duty than a real concern.

"I don't care. It needs to go to the cleaners anyway." So, the dry cleaners, not the closet. "And I need to kiss my wife."

I couldn't help the smile that appeared just as his mouth met mine. This man, after almost eight years together, still did it for me. Still made me giddy with a simple touch of his lips.

"I missed you," he said, cupping my cheek. He kissed me again, deeper this time, then sat back against the headboard with a content sigh.

That content sigh was a lie. If I really made him feel that way, why the hell did he need to introduce us to extracurricular sexual activities?

With perfect timing, JC looked down at my screen where The Open Door webpage was open in the corner, a reminder for myself that I wanted to talk about this later.

"Ah, you got my email!" He didn't sound the least bit sheepish. Rather, he sounded excited.

"Yeah. I got your email," I said dryly, my earlier emotions returning despite being beguiled by his kiss.

I set the laptop down on the bed and stood up, needing distance from his charm before addressing the issue. I folded my arms over my chest. "Am I supposed to be enthusiastic about it? Because I can assure you that I'm not."

JC's expression fell into his oh-shit-what-did-I-do-wrong look. I'd seen it plenty of times throughout our marriage, and even though we seemed to know each other pretty well now, it was surprising how often he still needed to wear it.

"Well," he said, cautiously, running a hand through his dark blond curls. "That wasn't the reaction I was expecting."

I was careful not to raise my voice, not only because I didn't want to wake the boys, but because I'd learned over the years that yelling didn't help these arguments. "Maybe you can tell me what you *were* expecting then. I mean, the price tag alone was enough to be intimidating."

His face relaxed with relief. "Oh, no. No. I didn't pay for the membership. I'd never spend that kind of money without talking to you." He slid my laptop aside so he could throw his legs over the side of the bed and perch on the edge. "Titus gave it to us. He said he was already a member and he'd gotten this as a gift. Which could be true." He shrugged.

I rolled my eyes. We both knew it was just as likely that Titus had flat-out bought it for my husband. Titus was the creator of one of the most successful apps that JC had invested in early on, and, now that he was a rich man himself, often co-invested in my husband's projects. I'd had the chance to meet him on several occasions. He had a very obvious crush on JC, but that hadn't stopped him from hitting on me at every opportunity. Despite his habit of injecting sexual overtones into every interaction, the guy was harmless. JC and I'd had more than a few laughs over him in the past.

The knowledge that he'd been the one to pay the exorbitant membership fee helped.

A little.

"Is the cost the only thing bothering you?" JC could read me well enough to see that it wasn't.

"No, it's not the only thing bothering me." I was mad, and I wanted to stay mad, but tears pricked at the corners of my eyes.

"Hey." JC reached out to rub my arm. When I dropped both of them by my side, he grabbed my hand and tugged me toward him. "What is it? Tell me how I hurt you."

I looked at his knees, unable to meet his eyes. "It just...it came as a surprise, honestly. I didn't know you felt this way."

"What way? How is it that you think I feel?" He stroked his hands up and down over my hips and thighs, coaxing the truth out of me.

I swallowed past the lump in my throat. I would not cry. I *would not* cry. "Are you not attracted to me anymore?" Somehow I managed not to let my voice crack as the question emerged from my mouth.

"Seriously? Are you kidding me?" He jumped to his feet and cradled my face between his hands. "Yes. Yes, I'm still attracted to you. You're the most beautiful creature on this planet. I'm so fucking in love with you. You know that. How can you not know that?"

My eyes flooded with water. "I know you love me. Of course you love me." We'd been through hell for each other, and, except for that time he got drunk and almost married another woman because he thought he'd lost me, oh, and that time he nearly stood me up at our own wedding, he'd shown me time and time again just how much he loved me. He adored me, actually. Treated me like a goddess.

And he was crazy for it.

"But look at me, JC. I have a C-section scar, my boobs are saggy from nursing. I weigh ten pounds more than I did when we were married, and I was three months pregnant at the time. I'm way past due for a hair appointment. I constantly smell like breast milk and spit-up. There's an eleven wrinkle forming between my brows, and my favorite jeans don't fit anymore and then my husband casually gets us a membership to an upper-class sex party. What other reason can there be than that I don't satisfy him anymore in the bedroom, and why would I when I look like this?"

He pulled me into him, his arms wrapped tightly around me, and I was pretty sure he was stifling a laugh. "You look amazing, Gwen," he said over my shoulder. "You're crazy to not see how addicted to your body I am. I can barely be in the same room with you without getting an erection, which has proved awkward on more than one occasion." He turned his head so his mouth was at my ear. "And all those supposed flaws you just listed? They make you even sexier. They remind me what you've done for me, things I could never do for you. Carried my babies in your body. Put up with me. My hair would be completely gray if I had to live with the likes of me."

I brought my palms up to his chest and pushed him gently back so I could look at his face. "Then why The Open Door? Just because Titus gave it to you didn't mean you had to accept it. And you've never mentioned wanting to do anything like that before. It makes me think you might feel like something's missing."

"Nothing's missing, baby. I promise." He weaved his fingers into the hair at the base of my skull as he kissed my temple. "I've heard you mention the club before, and I thought you might be interested in knowing more about it. That's all."

A new thought brought on a fresh wave of panic. "Did you think that *I* was bored in the bedroom? I've only ever been curious about it because it's so scandalous. That's all!"

"I know, I know," he said reassuringly, his expression saying it was ridiculous that I ever thought otherwise. "Who wouldn't be curious? And I could have told Titus thanks, but no thanks and then just tell you, hey, guess what really exists and leave it at that. But if I'd done that, I'd be denying you the opportunity to take advantage of a membership that you might find very satisfying."

I scowled. Had he just given me the I-did-it-for-you excuse?

"Don't look at me that way," he said, correctly assessing my expression. "All I'm saying is that, while I am perfectly happy and content to never change a thing in our sex life, I also know that pushing your boundaries is a real turn-on for you."

I felt my cheeks redden. It was weird how I could still flush when talking about these things with him. He had always been so forward, so direct, and I'd always been reluctant to speak openly about sex and the things I wanted from it.

But he was right. I had always liked my boundaries pushed. And he'd always known exactly how to guide me through experimentation. He'd shown me that I liked mutual masturbation and the idea of getting caught and butt plugs and anal, all things I never would have tried if he hadn't known better than I did that they were what I wanted.

But I didn't want to share my husband. I didn't want to watch him with someone else.

Did I?

"I'm not suggesting we swap with another couple or anything," he said, reading my mind. "I'd have to murder anyone who even tried to put his hands on you." His voice dropped to a timbre that was thick and sultry. "But we could watch."

A shiver ran through me even though I suddenly felt incredibly warm.

JC ran his fingers sensually up and down my back. "Letting strangers see how good I can make you feel, showing them how sexy you look when you come, making sure they know the whole time that you're mine and only mine…"

He trailed off, letting the fantasy form in my mind.

"That's hot," I said, panting.

"So hot," he agreed with heavily lidded eyes.

"But…" I said, trying to hold the thought before it got lost to lust. "Is that something people like us do? Regular people. With kids. Do moms just get a sitter on a Saturday night so they can go watch strangers fuck?"

His brows moved together in a crease. "Does it matter what other people do?" He let a beat pass for me to ponder. "Remember when we first got back together? Not the first time, I mean the second time." He had to clarify since there had been a year break in our initial romance due to circumstances beyond our control.

I gave him an incredulous look, because duh. Our love story was the most important story of my life, and, yeah, I remembered it.

"Okay, well, what do you remember about how we navigated that?"

"I remember that you thought I'd be better off without you and you ghosted me right before our wedding." It wasn't where he was going with this, obviously, but I never failed to take an opportunity to remind him of his momentary stupidity.

"Hey, I came back in time to say my vows," he said, pinching my thigh in retribution for the reminder. "That's not what I'm talking about and you know it. Do you remember before that? When you worried things were moving too fast and that we shouldn't jump into bed together so soon, shouldn't move in with each other so soon, shouldn't—"

I finished for him. "Get married so soon. Yes, I remember that." Suddenly I knew where he was going. "And you said fuck everyone else, we have to do things the way that's right for us."

"Yes. *Our* way. And if going to kinky parties is our thing, then we should do it. It doesn't change what we have or what we are to our kids. It's just—"

"Our way," I said with him.

We'd made a good life doing things *our way*. Why was I doubting it now?

I couldn't examine that answer at the moment, because JC seemed to want my help in reminding me what *our way* usually entailed—being naked. He tugged on the hem of my T-shirt and I raised my arms so he could pull it over my head. As I began to work the buttons of his dress shirt, he brought his hand to cup my bare breast. Then he brought his mouth toward mine.

"Think about it," he said after licking along the curve of my lower lip. "We can check it out, or we can forget it even exists. It's completely up to you."

Then conversation ceased as he devoured me with his mouth, stroking his thumb across my sensitive nipple while I wrestled with getting his cock out of his pants.

And I would think about it more—the club, the opportunity to push boundaries, the need to do things that were right for us instead of others.

But, currently, I had better things to focus on. The kids were sleeping, the house was quiet, and my sexy-as-fuck husband was worshiping my baby-worn body, proving that nothing was missing between us at all.

Chapter Three

The sex had just started getting good when Jake called out for *Mommy*.

We tried to ignore him, hoping at least one of us could get to a climax before our five-year-old got out of bed and came looking for us.

But his call persisted, his tone getting more and more frantic, and soon the baby was awake and crying too. Whatever progress my orgasm had made was lost in the chaos.

With a sigh, JC and I threw clothes on and split our parenting tasks. I went for Braden, who was teething and probably just needed some baby Anbesol and a quick comfort feed. JC got the short end of the stick, it turned out, because Jake had woken up with a tummy ache, and by the time his father reached him, he'd thrown up all over himself and his bed.

Needless to say, it was a long night for all of us.

Maybe that was why The Open Door was the first thing on my mind when I awoke from the three hour "nap" I managed to get in the early hours of the morning. The one thing a sex club like that could offer was a kid-free environment. Of course, we could get that just by hiring a babysitter and getting a hotel for a night. These days, though, I wasn't sure that JC and I wouldn't just use that time to catch up on our sleep. And, thanks to Titus, this was already paid for.

The Open Door could push us to give attention to our sex life—to *us*—and while our relationship was pretty solid for the most part, there couldn't be any harm in making sure we stayed that way.

And sex was vital between my husband and me. It was how JC and I had first connected. We'd had a no-strings arrangement for several months, an arrangement that quickly turned complicated when feelings got involved. Regardless, our initial draw to each other had been through physical intimacy, and, as much as I wanted to deny it, we really had let that aspect of our relationship slip in the past couple of years. The Open Door might be just the answer.

But was that the best way to address the issue? Inviting strangers into our love life? Possibly encountering new challenges and jealousies?

Problems like this were best discussed with a friend. Luckily, I had a date with my *best* friend that very morning.

So, exhausted as I was, I forced myself out of bed and into the shower while JC took the first round of kid-wrangling.

* * * *

"I'm sorry," I said when Alayna met me at the elevator of her penthouse. It was pretty obvious what I was apologizing for. The plan had been for me to come over sans kids. Alayna wasn't only my friend, but also my co-manager—technically, my boss—but she was still on maternity leave after the birth of her twins, and I hadn't seen her in a while.

I'd desperately been looking forward to a day off from momming, but when that didn't work out, I wasn't about to cancel my date with my friend.

"No worries," Alayna said. She shifted her own sleeping baby to one arm and reached for Theo. The nanny arrived just then to take her infant off to the nursery.

"I'm sorry," I said again, setting the diaper bag and the carrier on the floor before bending down to unbuckle the child inside. "JC was going to watch all of them. Since we both have Mondays off, we don't have the nanny, but then Jake got sick, so JC had to take him to the doctor, and here I am, schlepping kids over to your house." I paused and smiled as I really looked at my baby. "Hey, look at that. Braden's asleep too."

"I'll put the carrier in the nursery then," the nanny said, returning for the next batch of kids. She grabbed the handle of the baby carrier in one hand and held her other hand out for Theo, enticing him to accompany her with the promise of puzzles.

"We have so many babies," Alayna groaned, with a tired look that likely matched my own. "How did this happen?"

"I keep asking myself the same thing. But they're so cute." We both had three kids that we loved with all our being, but at least I'd had mine one at a time. Alayna had decided to follow her first daughter with twins.

Which was one of the main reasons why she was still on leave almost a year after they'd been born, and I'd been back since Braden had been four months. Well, and she'd had some health issues too, both before and after their birth. I was lucky in that department. While I seemed to get pregnant at the drop of my husband's pants, at least I had easy-breezy pregnancies. Even the recovery from my C-section with Theo hadn't been too rough.

"We could've rescheduled, you know," Alayna said, as I trailed after her into the living room. She plopped down on the sofa. "Today wasn't urgent."

She said that, but I could tell she was glad I'd come. She was getting restless at home and found herself thinking more and more about work. I knew she'd invited me over to help her brainstorm some ideas for the future of the club as much as to just hang out.

"I know it's not urgent, but I need your advice, and I didn't want to talk about this by text." I sat down on the opposite end of the sofa, twisting so my back was against the arm, and I was facing her. "And I definitely didn't want to talk about this by phone in case Hudson was around."

I liked her husband enough—he was a little strange, but he'd become family. That didn't mean I wanted to discuss my sex life with him. Sure, Alayna would probably tell him everything later on—she was adamant they had no secrets—and that was fine. I just didn't want to be there for it.

Alayna's eyebrows rose. "Geez, way to pique my curiosity. Hit me. The doctor is in."

"Okay." Now, how did I go about presenting this? I brought my hands together like I was praying and put them up to my mouth as I tried to gather my thoughts. "Okay," I said after a few silent beats, no closer to a beginning than I'd been the first time I uttered the two syllables.

Her jaw suddenly fell slack. "Oh, fuck, you're not pregnant, are you?"

"No! God, no. I'm still breastfeeding Braden." Although with my history, that didn't mean anything. I'd gotten pregnant with Jake while I had an IUD and then gotten pregnant again while I'd been nursing him. The second pregnancy had ended in miscarriage before I'd even known I'd been knocked up. I hadn't even had a period yet.

"Then what is it?"

Having found a place to start, I took a breath and dove in. "Remember how last year Mirabelle told us she'd heard about these sex parties around town? The anonymous, masquerade, private kink parties that required exclusive invites because most of the guests were elite upper class, important people? Famous people? People that don't want their kinks in the gossip columns?"

"Yes, but you know half of what she hears from her clients is bullshit rumors."

"Right, right." Her sister-in-law owned a fashion boutique and was definitely privy to more socialite gossip than either of us. "But. This time, the rumor isn't so much a rumor anymore. JC got an invite." I felt my blood get warmer just at the mention of the club.

"What." The word came out more astonished than questioning.

"Yep. Exactly what I said." I stroked my palms up and down my thighs, feeling fidgety with nervous energy. "This guy who sometimes co-invests in projects with JC got us the invitation. Honestly, I think he has a thing for my husband—maybe for both of us? And is probably hoping for a threesome, which JC said no way to already. Not that I asked! He doesn't share, and neither do I, but you don't have to have sex if you go to one of these things."

Her expression was still stunned. "You mean, you could just go and...watch?"

"Yeah. Just watch. Like a live porno." I could feel my cheeks go red. Was this something people admitted to being into? Was I crossing some friend line, exposing myself as a pervert to an innocent friend?

But then her eyes glazed. "That's hot," she said with a dreamy sigh.

I let out the breath I'd been holding. Thank God she didn't think I was a giant sex freak. "So hot. JC thinks so too."

"Are you going to go?" she asked eagerly, like it was something I definitely should be considering.

Perhaps she was more progressive than I was because it had taken me longer to get to that phase. And I still didn't have a solid answer.

"I don't know!" I exclaimed in exasperation. "That's why I need your advice."

"Let's talk it through. Pros and cons. Pros—go."

It was strange to have her be the voice of reason. Usually, I was good at being rational and would have made a pro/con list first thing.

Fortunately, I'd started thinking through it while I'd been in the shower. "It would be fun, an experience, spice up our love life—not that it needs it." I was reassuring myself more than her. "Could learn some new tricks. Make me feel young. Could meet new people."

"Those are great. What are the cons?"

"I hate people. Why would I want to meet more of them?"

I smiled at her laugh, but as soon as she fell silent again, I grew somber. Because the cons, though few, were hard to say. They revealed my insecurities as a wife. As a woman. "What if JC was attracted to another woman? All those hot naked girls in front of him?"

"He's always dealt with business around naked women, and he's only ever had eyes for you." She shrugged dismissively while somehow still making me feel like she was taking me seriously.

It made it easier to say more. "I've popped three babies out. I have a scar from my C-section. Two words: stretch marks."

"Pfft. You know how devoted that man is to you."

"Yeah. I do." But that didn't mean I should tempt fate.

Or was it worse to not take this opportunity? What if my adventurous husband eventually got bored because I didn't feel confident enough to take these kinds of risks?

"Do you *want* to go to a kinky sex party?" she asked after I'd been quiet for too long.

Yes. I did.

But I didn't want that to be the wrong answer.

But I really did want to go. The more I thought about it, the more the fantasy came to life in my head, the more my curiosity bloomed.

But what if we went and someone found out? Or someone we knew saw us there?

I threw myself back with a frustrated sigh. "This is stupid, isn't it? I shouldn't even be entertaining the idea."

She scowled at me. "Why the hell not?"

"I'm a respectable woman. I'm a mother of three. I should be responsible."

"That's right, you are a respectable woman." Her tone was fierce and energized, and I knew before she went on that she was launching into one of her typical passionate Alayna Pierce sermons. "And *because* you respect yourself, you should give yourself what you want. You should do something for yourself—and your husband. Something that isn't at all about your identity as a mother. Is that really all you exist for now? To feed and clothe and protect and shuttle around these little humans? Yes, they're important, but if you start acting like the only part of yourself that you're obligated to is your motherly side, you're not going to be any good for them. You need to be a complete person, whole and entire, and, by damn, that means going to a sex party and watching other people kink it up if that's what fills your cup."

She made it sound so easy. Was it really that easy?

Yeah. I was pretty sure it was.

I folded my arms and smiled at her. "Thank you. I knew that, but I needed to hear it."

"And I need you to go to a party and tell me all the details after."

I laughed. "I'm still getting up the nerve, but, for sure, if I go, I'll tell you everything."

It was a lie. I'd already made my decision. She was right—if I wanted to go, I should go, and I definitely wanted to go. Not to do anything, but just to check it out. See what all the fuss was about.

And I would tell Alayna about it, eventually.

First, I needed to tell my husband.

Chapter Four

While JC had assured me that going to The Open Door was my decision, I knew he'd be excited when I said yes. Which was why I wanted to make it special when I told him. He was the kind of guy who could turn ordinary occasions into something remarkable, and he was often surprising me with the effort he made to celebrate the simple things.

I wanted to do that for him.

Since this was the beginning of a journey to invest in our relationship, it seemed fitting to mark the event somehow. Considering we had three young ones, no babysitter, and one of them sick with strep throat according to the clinic's rapid test, finding a way to fit "special" into our life was a bit of a challenge.

But I wouldn't be deterred.

After the kids had been fed and bathed and then re-bathed when I discovered puke in Jake's hair and more black marker on Theo, JC and I split up for bedtime. I was the only one with the boobs so I got Braden. For once, the baby was easy. He'd been lugged around with me all day, which seemed to have worn him out.

As I snuck out of his room, I could hear Theo and Jake begging JC for "one more story." That meant I had time. Not a lot of time, but enough to dash to the master suite, freshen up and change into something sexy.

Of course it took four lingerie changes before I found a teddy that still fit and didn't make my stomach hang over the panties like the top of a muffin. Thankfully JC was the one of us who really got into storytelling, reading all the characters in different voices with enthusiastic expression.

Even so, I'd just finished with the flat iron and a fresh coat of mascara before I heard him coming down the hall. Quickly, I threw myself on the bed and propped myself up on my elbows, jutting my milk-swollen breasts out, hoping I looked more sexy than awkward.

He was taking off his T-shirt as he entered the room, so I got a view of his still-magnificently chiseled abs before he spotted me. Instantly I was wet.

At least getting aroused wasn't an issue for us.

"I changed two times today, and I swear I still smell like vomit," he said through the cotton material. Then the shirt was over his head, and he saw me. He stopped suddenly, his eyes clouding as a smile spread across his lips. "Well, well. That's sure a nice view."

He dropped the garment on the floor and moved to stand before me at the side of the bed. Bending down to trail his fingers up my shin—thank goodness I'd done a quick shave that morning in the shower—he said, "Two nights in a row. What did I do to deserve this?"

I winced inwardly at the statement. There had been a time when we never missed a night of sex. Now we were still frequent with our lovemaking, but consecutive nights were definitely a rarity. And I wasn't even sure the night before even counted, since neither of us got to a release.

That's why this is a good decision, I said to myself. We were good together, but we had been better. We could be better again.

"Come find out," I answered, teasingly, beckoning him to cover my body with his. I wanted to feel the weight of him over me, wanted to feel him between my legs. He wanted it too. I could already make out the thick outline of his cock through his jeans.

But instead of laying himself over me, he continued drawing his fingers over my skin, leaving bursts of goosebumps in their wake.

"JC," I begged.

"I'll get there. Patience." He bent down to kiss the sensitive spot on my inner knee, then followed it up with a kiss a little higher on the inside of my thigh.

God, this was delicious torture. He could do this all night, and I'd be happy.

At the same time, a clock ticked urgently inside my head. How long would we have before getting interrupted? Shouldn't we try to hurry this up?

"Don't you dare rush me," he said, reading my thoughts, before moving his mouth to leave kisses higher on the inside of my leg. Higher still. Then at the crease where my legs met my torso. Then on top of the crotch panel of my panties.

My breath hitched as his lips found my clit through the thin material. "Yesssss," I hissed.

"You like that?" he asked, not because he didn't already know that I did, but because he liked hearing it.

"I do like it. I love it."

He continued to suck and nip at the sensitive bud, undoing the button and zipper of his jeans at the same time. Without pausing what he was doing with his mouth, he pushed his jeans down his legs and stepped first one foot then the other out of them.

Then, dressed only in a pair of dark gray boxer briefs, he stretched out over me, and took my mouth with his.

While he kissed me, he shifted more to his side so he could reach down again to massage my throbbing pussy. I moaned against his lips as his strokes went from languid to rough, the beginnings of an orgasm building under his skilled touch.

"I like this," he said, pulling away to gaze down at the sheer material of my nightie. His voice rumbled low in his throat, sending a shiver through my body. "You're so sexy. The sexiest woman alive."

Sure. Fine.

But if there was actually anything sexy about me, it was because he made me feel that way.

He kissed me again, his tongue sliding between my lips to lick at the roof of my mouth. "I'd be completely content if you wore this all the time. Or nothing at all. I'm not picky." His mouth devoured my giggle, and his finger increased the pressure on my clit. "But I have to know—does this have anything to do with last night's topic of conversation?"

My cheeks flushed. "Yes."

One brow rose as he looked down at me inquisitively. "You don't have to prove anything, Gwen."

"Not in that way. That's not what I meant. I didn't…" But didn't I kind of? Didn't I dress up in a skimpy outfit to tell him about my decision so that I could simultaneously justify that this sex club thing was just for fun, and not because we had any problem finding the spark on our own?

No, that wasn't the main reason I'd done this.

I brought my hand up to graze affectionately through the short trimmed stubble of his beard. He'd adopted it recently, and while it had taken a little bit to get used to, I'd found I loved the rugged scratch of his beard between my thighs when he went down on me. Needless to say, I hoped he never shaved it again.

"JC," I said, reassuring him. "It's not what you think. I wanted to let you know that I spent all day thinking about The Open Door. All last night too, since we were up for most of it. And I want to go. If you do." He hadn't really given his opinion on the matter. "Do you want to go?"

His hand settled between my thighs, his sweet caress momentarily abandoned. "I'm interested. But not if it's going to make you feel inferior or like you aren't enough for me or that you have to be a better seductress or whatever this is that you're doing."

"I don't feel that way. I know we're good. And the seduction routine? I seriously was just excited about making this decision to deepen our physical connection, and I wanted to start right away. Like, tonight." I leaned up to kiss him. "Is that okay?"

"It's very okay." He resumed petting me. Then stopped again. "I need to say something for the record, though. I do want to go to this club with you. Not because I think we aren't good together the way we are, but because I think we're fucking awesome together. And I want to have every fucking awesome experience with you possible. And this has the potential to be really fucking awesome. And if it's not, we never go again."

"That sounds like a perfect plan." I leaned up again to tease his lips. "And now do you think you could maybe go back to the fucking awesome experience that was about to happen between my legs?"

He chuckled, but he did as I asked, rubbing me closer to climax. I could feel it growing inside me, winding tighter and tighter and tighter until—

"Mommy's making weird noises," a tiny voice croaked from the foot of the bed.

Shit! We'd forgotten to lock the door.

I scrambled to cover myself up with a pillow, glad that we hadn't yet lost all our clothes, while JC sat up casually, bending over as he did so that his erection wasn't visible.

"Hey, Jake, buddy. We didn't see you. Are you feeling bad again? Is it time for some more medicine?"

My five-year-old shook his head, his blond curls bouncing as he did. "Theo puked."

I brought my hand to my face and groaned.

"I'll take care of it," JC said and began climbing over me to retrieve his pants.

I grabbed his arm to stop him. "No. It's my turn. You did the last clean-up."

"And I'm doing this one too." When I started to protest again, he cut me off. "I'm already up. You stay here and keep the bed warm." He bowed down to whisper in my ear. "And keep those thoughts naughty. I'll be back to finish this."

But he didn't come back.

He disappeared down the dark hall with Jacob, and when I went to check on him after he hadn't returned an hour later, I found him asleep in the rocking chair with our Theo nestled in his arms.

I sighed as I covered them up with a blanket and kissed both of their foreheads then went back to my empty bed, where I fell asleep dreaming of what possibilities awaited us at The Open Door.

Chapter Five

According to the schedule of events on The Open Door website, parties occurred weekly on Saturday nights. The location varied, primarily taking place in homes of senior members, members not averse to sharing their address. Locations varied from down the street from us to an hour or two away. While distance would normally play a deciding role in which we chose to attend, this time it was our availability. Our calendar was full and, with a previous engagement already on the books, JC and I couldn't attend that coming Saturday when the event was nearby. So we chose to go to one far away, not wanting to wait another week, and it was a full twelve days between deciding and actually going.

Twelve days gave me lots of time to think about it. Too much time, JC would probably have said. I didn't ever change my mind about going, but I chose and re-chose my outfit more than twenty times, and, even though neither of us wanted to wear an optional mask, I questioned that decision daily.

I debated about my scheduled shift at The Sky Launch, too. I usually left work at six on Saturdays, and the party didn't start until ten, but was that enough time to get ready? Would I be too tired after work to go out? Would I be too eager to care?

Then there were the discussions on boundaries. Every night at bedtime I made sure we were on the same page. "No touching anyone else and no one touches us," I'd say.

"Absolutely no touching," JC would say in agreement.

"If we change our mind about that in the future, that's fine, but we're not allowed to change our mind *during* a party. It has to be discussed beforehand."

"Has to be discussed beforehand."

I went through it so often that JC's responses became rote, basically repeating whatever I'd said with a nod of his head. The more he parroted what I said, the more I feared he wasn't really listening to me, that he wasn't authentically committing, and so I'd go over it again. It was a vicious cycle that had both of us snapping at each other by the end of the second week.

Then it was Saturday, the day we'd decided to attend, and instead of being the anxious ball of nerves that I'd been winding toward, a charged calm settled over me. I was excited and tranquil all at once. I'd researched as much as I could, and still had no idea what we were in for, and that was okay. I was going to let it be fun.

The party this week was an hour outside Manhattan in Greenwich, Connecticut. Normally we used public transportation and Ubers for our day-to-day travel needs, and while we did seriously consider taking an Uber, JC ended up pulling our rarely-driven BMW out of the garage for the journey. I'd saved putting on my makeup for the ride so I'd have something to focus on, something that wasn't wondering what the hell we were in store for. It was a well-thought-out distraction, for the most part, despite the dwindling daylight. Thank goodness for lighted mirrors.

The sun was completely gone when we pulled up to the address indicated on the GPS, a two-story manor house with a stone wall and plenty of acreage.

"I'm going to park down the road a bit," JC said when he saw the lavish circle driveway packed with cars. "In case we need to make a quick getaway."

I laughed but was glad we were on the same page.

He parked and got out of the car, hurrying over to help me out of my side. Once I was standing next to him, my stiletto heels bringing me nearer than usual to his six foot height, he drew his eyes over me, slowly. I'd chosen to wear a ballet pink midi dress with a draped skirt that knotted at the neck. I hadn't wanted to be too exposed on my first visit to the club, but I'd simultaneously worried I hadn't dressed sexy enough.

JC's heavy gaze convinced me I'd chosen just fine.

"You look stunning," he said, almost surprised, as though he'd just looked at me for the first time that night. It was a very real possibility considering the hustle and bustle there'd been turning the kids over to my brother and getting out of the house.

I hadn't really looked at him, either, and I did so now, giving him as much attention as he'd given me as I took in his dark blue Armani suit. The jacket was double-breasted and tailored, but he'd paired it with a multi-shaded blue button-down that gave him a casually classy look. He'd always been able to wear a suit like a god, and this occasion was no different, but I was taken aback by how long it had been since I'd noticed that. When was the last time I'd truly looked at this man? Truly appreciated him? I sort of took him for granted these days, and the realization stung.

"What's the matter?" he asked when I'd stared too long without speaking. "Should I have worn something else?"

I blinked out of my reverie. "Nope. You're perfect." Before I could get too sappy, I grabbed his hand in mine and started tugging him down the street. "Now let's get inside so I can show you off."

We walked a total of two steps before a terrible thought occurred to me, bringing me to an abrupt halt. "Titus! Is he going to be there? Is that going to be weird?"

JC's expression, which had gone into worried mode when I'd stopped, relaxed. "No, thank God. He left last week for Europe for a big project for a year. There could be other people we know, though..."

"I know." I'd tried not to think about it, and still didn't want to now. "We'll deal with that when we have to. I'm just glad I don't have to worry about Titus trying to get his paws all over my man." Like, what if he thought our acceptance of the invitation was an acceptance of something more? What if he thought we owed him?

"Not happening," JC reassured me. "Even if he were here. Let me go on to assure you that no man is getting his paws all over your man."

That mollified me. Though I didn't miss that he hadn't said anything about the paws of women.

The house was in one of the wealthiest areas of the country, and, if the myriad of Jags, Cadillacs, and Porsches in the driveway indicated, the members of The Open Door were equally of means. We had money because JC had been born with that privilege, but I'd come from poverty and was still a penny pincher. I had simple needs and even the most extravagant of my wants could be afforded on my salary alone. That aspect of the current environment made me feel out of place, and for the first time since I'd said yes, I started to doubt myself.

"It's not too late to turn back," my intuitive husband said as we reached the top of the front steps. "Last chance."

I considered for the length of a deep breath. "I don't want to turn back. I want to see what this is all about." The sign posted on the door invited members to just walk in, and JC reached his hand out toward the knob, when I added, "And remember—"

"No touching of others, no touching of us. I got it, babe. Trust me." He kissed me on the side of the mouth then opened the door, and there we were, guests at our first sex party.

Immediately, it was like no other party I'd been to. A man in a butler's outfit—a man I was pretty certain wasn't actually a butler—checked our names and ID to be sure we were members then sent us to a table that had been set up in the foyer where a woman in a French maid's outfit took our cell phones.

"What color?" she asked, gesturing to three separate colors of paper wrist bracelets in front of her.

Shit if I knew.

I looked to JC. "What does each color stand for?" he asked, somehow managing to sound like we'd just forgotten rather than like we were clueless.

"Red means you've already consented to physical compliments and non-sexual touch as a means of initiation. Black means that verbal consent is required before anyone touches or compliments you. The white means you'd prefer to initiate any interaction."

"White," JC and I said in unison.

With a bored sigh, she tore off two white bracelets and wrote a number on one of them before she handed them to us. "That's your claim number for your cell phones. If you'd like a guided initiation, talk to Ang over there." She nodded toward a transgender woman down the hall who was dressed like an angel, complete with wings and a halo.

"Thanks." JC grabbed the bracelets and put his hand to the small of my back, ushering me away from the maid. "We don't need a—?"

I answered before he finished asking the question. "No. I'd prefer to initiate ourselves, I think."

"Same." He took my hand and placed the paper wristband around it before bringing it up to kiss my palm. "So let's get initiating, shall we?"

I waited for him to put on his own band then linked my arm in his, urging him to lead the way.

Without a guide, we couldn't know for sure what areas were off limits, if any, but there were several rooms accessible from the foyer that appeared to be available. JC chose to steer us to the right, into a formal living room. There was a sofa and loveseat that I imagined were permanent fixtures as well as several mismatched chairs circling the perimeter, like it was book club night and the owners of the house needed to accommodate the extra guests. In other words, very ordinary.

That was where the ordinary stopped.

The space was filled with people in various states of undress. Some were making out. Some were humping with all their clothes on. Some were naked but just talking. The group sitting on the floor in front of the couch were in a massage line, each rubbing the back of the person in front of them. One man was doing a striptease for the three onlookers sitting on the loveseat. Next to us a foursome tickled each other with long peacock feathers, and, in the corner, a large group sat in a circle, masturbating.

A queen-size mattress had been placed in the center of the room, and a trio of women dressed in burlesque outfits were kissing and petting there. We watched them from the doorway until a couple nearby vacated the armchair and gestured to JC for us to take it.

"Was that…?" I whispered, my eyes following the tall dark-skinned male half of the pair.

"Pretty sure, yeah."

I didn't know sports figures by name, but this one was familiar enough that I recognized his face. And frame. And those perfectly sculpted biceps. And his tight, tight…

JC tugged me sharply down onto his lap. "Would you rather follow after them?" he whispered in my ear.

"Uh…" Yes? Was that an option? But also, no. Because I was already on the verge of being overstimulated. "I'm happy right here," I said, not quite sure happy was the right word. Intrigued was more appropriate. Fascinated.

We sat together, watching the women as they shed their clothing and moved past foreplay to breast play. Or I pretended to watch them. While I caught the gist of what they were doing, I snuck more glances around the room, blushing and turning quickly away every time someone caught me staring. It felt wrong. Naughty. Yet, a few seconds later, my head would twist again and my eyes would fix on something new and exciting and taboo.

There were so many sights to behold, so many images. The man with the penis pierced in not one, but two places. The woman treating the man at her feet like he was her dog. The man at her feet who kept barking and panting. There was no way I'd remember everything to be able to report back to Alayna. Some of it was sexy, for sure—the two men going down on the woman on the couch was pretty hot. A lot of it, though, was just too...different.

One of the women on the mattress had just (incredibly) orgasmed from having her tits sucked and nothing else when JC nuzzled my ear. "I'd like to try another room when you're up for it."

"Ready now."

The next room seemed to be a toy room of sorts. There were spanking benches and rings hanging from the ceiling with ropes threaded through them and one of those X shaped crosses. An assortment of riding crops and whips were laid out next to a basket of wet wipes, condoms and lube. In the center of the room was a gadget that looked a lot like a saddle except it had a remote control that made it vibrate in different ways. A gray-haired woman sat on it while an equally elderly man played with the dials, changing the speed and rhythm of the vibration of the saddle. A second, younger woman stood behind the contraption, striking the older woman repeatedly with a flogger.

It took exactly two minutes before JC and I turned in unison and walked out. Apparently neither of us were into pain with our sex.

"Maybe it's something that you have to really *try* to understand? Maybe it grows on you." I thought I should at least give it the benefit of the doubt.

"Not interested," JC said with finality. Well, now I knew.

The next room we walked into was dark, the only light coming from the hallway. I could make out a naked man lying face down on a massage table in the middle of the space, and an Asian woman standing to the side. A crowd of people were gathered so, out of curiosity, JC and I joined them. After a few minutes, it appeared that what we were witnessing was a simple rub-down.

Except then the masseuse picked up a wand with a handle on one end and some sort of cloth ball at the other. She dipped it into a bucket of what looked like water, which I realized was really alcohol, because when she brought a lighter to it, it lit up with fire. She then took the torch and swiped it over the man's back. Her other hand followed the path of the torch, rubbing the heat into his skin. The fire didn't last long, but as soon as it went out, she repeated the process.

After this went on for awhile, with me flinching the entire time, the masseuse brought a second wand out. This one she dipped in the alcohol, but she didn't light it. Instead she drew a shape on the man's back with the alcohol, then, with the first wand, she lit the shape on fire.

"Oh, my God," I gasped, clapping my hand over my mouth too late. A few people near us chuckled at my reaction. I could feel my cheeks heat like they were the ones on fire.

We stayed for a little while longer, but then the therapist started lighting glass cups and putting them rim down on the man's back, and I was ready to leave.

"They offer cupping at my day spa," I said as I tugged JC out into the hall. "If I decide I want to do it one day, I don't need a bunch of strangers watching."

We stopped at the bottom of the stairs. There was another room on this floor, but we could hear noise coming from above us as well. JC gave me a questioning look.

I was torn. It seemed quieter upstairs, which made it appealing, but also scarier. I had a feeling it was a whole other level up there, literally and figuratively. Excited voices coming from the next room provided the deciding factor. As much as I longed for a less crowded space, I was drawn by curiosity.

This room seemed to be a library with bookshelves along three of the walls. It wasn't lined with chairs along the perimeter like the first room. Instead, it had pillows. Stacks and stacks of giant pillows. In the center of the room, a woman in a wrap dress and heels stood with a man wearing black dress pants and a black sweater who was holding a small tool bag and a roll of duct tape in the other. He held the tape up and addressed the audience.

"I prefer something softer for beginners—neckties or satin scarves," he said. "But if you and your partner are ready to push to the next level, duct tape and zip ties can offer another level of realism to the fantasy."

A binding demonstration sounded kind of hot. I'd daydreamed about being tied up before. This was definitely interesting.

We found an unoccupied spot on the floor and settled in to watch whatever was about to play out, expecting the man to show different methods and materials to use when binding someone else.

Instead, when he'd finished talking about the tape, he dropped it in his bag, hiked it up over his shoulder and said they were ready to get started.

The room fell to a hush as the man came and crouched in the corner near us. The woman took a book off the bookshelf and began walking around the space, pretending to be reading as she did. Without a glance toward her scene partner, she passed by us. I was so distracted watching what she'd do next, I didn't notice the man leave us to stalk behind her until he'd grabbed her.

Instantly, she screamed. A real-life blood-curdling scream. The man clapped his hand over her mouth. She struggled—really struggled. She kicked and bit and flailed. But he fought just as hard. Convincingly hard. She was going to be bruised when this was over. Was that sexy?

When he slapped her hard across the jaw, I started to wonder if someone should stop him. I looked from JC to the people sitting next to us to the people sitting across from us.

"It's rape play," said a voluptuous woman at my side.

"Oh." I wasn't so naïve as to have never heard of the thing, but I'd always envisioned rape play as frisky struggling in bed. Where the woman would say, "Stop," and "No," and then giggle because they both knew she didn't mean it.

I hadn't expected there to be an actual physical altercation.

I couldn't decide how I felt about it, watching this man literally hold her down, binding her wrists and covering her mouth with duct tape from the tool bag—his "rape kit," apparently. All the while, she screamed and wailed as he said things like, "I only like it more when you cry," and "If you bite my cock, I'll break your neck."

It was too real. Disturbingly real. Make-my-skin-crawl real.

And yet, it was also arousing.

I was keenly aware of the dampness of my panties and my beaded nipples brushing across the material of my dress as my chest rose and fell with jittery breaths.

I couldn't even look at JC. I didn't want to know what he thought about the display. And there was absolutely no fucking way I'd let him know I was turned on.

Once the woman was sufficiently bound, the man literally tore her dress off her, the ripping sound causing someone next to me to let out an awed gasp. I didn't know who. I couldn't tear my eyes off the scene to look as he forcefully fucked the woman, smacking her when she tried to claw at him. Holding her in place when she tried to get away. Putting his hands around her throat when she screamed too loud behind the tape.

Somehow, despite her protestations, the woman managed to orgasm. Not once, but three times, from what I could tell. Though that didn't necessarily mean anything since I had learned once that women could get wet and sometimes even orgasm from real rape, despite not wanting it to happen to them. Nevertheless, when the scene was over and the audience applauded, this woman appeared so satiated that she glowed.

"Whoa," JC said quietly behind me, a single syllable that didn't give me any indication of whether it was a good whoa or a bad whoa or a what-the-hell-did-I-just watch whoa.

"Whoa," I repeated with the same ambiguousness.

We continued to watch as they cleaned up. JC winced when the man pulled the duct tape off her mouth. She got out of the bindings at her wrist by herself, which was oddly fascinating. I'd always thought duct tape was the impenetrable fix-all, but all she did was raise her arms above her head then drop them really fast, shooting her elbows to the side, and the tape broke clean through.

At that, I finally looked at my husband, "*How cool was that?*" poised on my lips. The words stuck in my mouth, though, when I saw the uneasy look he wore and the pale color of his face.

"I'm ready to leave," he said, pulling me up with him as he stood. "If that's okay."

"Yeah. Okay," I said, not quite certain this was the note I wanted to end the night on.

On the other hand, the rape scene had been the most intriguing portion of the evening, and it had also been the most discomforting. If there was anything left at the party to pique my curiosity, I wasn't sure I wanted to know.

Chapter Six

Without a word, we headed back to the foyer and collected our phones. We didn't touch or speak as we walked back to the car, the weight of everything we'd just seen and experienced pressing heavy between us. There was so much to process. So many kinks I'd only ever read about. So many more I'd never heard of at all.

It was overwhelming.

I didn't know where to begin to organize my own emotions, let alone understand what JC was feeling.

It was obvious he was trying to sort it all out in his head. He had the furrow in his forehead he always got when he was thinking intensely, and he didn't even attempt to come open my car door, a move he never would have missed if he hadn't been distracted.

I respected his need to process on his own—JC had always been a sensitive man and frequently needed bouts of solitude to wade through the gravity of all he felt. I'd learned to give him his time, learned to sit quietly at his side or leave him to brood alone over his piano until he came out of his reverie.

But this time I was feeling things too. I didn't know if I could handle an entire ride back to the City in such thick silence.

On the other hand, I didn't have any idea what to say to break the tension.

Inside the car, JC tossed the key fob into the cup holder, and I absentmindedly reached for my seatbelt, searching for an entrance to conversation. But, after several seconds, he still hadn't made a move to push the button to start the engine.

With my hand clasped around the belt, poised to pull across my lap, I paused to scrutinize his profile.

"Well," he said, staring out the window into the black night in front of him. "That was enlightening."

I let go of the belt, tentatively relieved he'd broken the ice. "That's one word for it." There were a bunch of other words to add—confusing, amazing, shocking, arousing. But like hell was I going to be the first one to say more.

"I thought I was a fairly open-minded guy—and I am. Thumbs up to people getting off on what they like. But...wow. Not sure I ever needed to see some of that."

I nodded. "It sure puts the things we do in perspective. Anal is, like, boring comparatively."

He laughed. He had to remember the first time he introduced me to a butt plug. I'd been plenty freaked, only to discover afterward that it was one of my favorite sexual pleasures. I'd felt progressive then, sexually.

Boy, had I been naïve.

"Did you see that guy with his dick pierced?" he asked, throwing a glance in my direction.

"It was pierced *twice!*"

"I don't even want to imagine."

"Ouch." We both grimaced in unison.

"Do you think it really makes a difference to the woman?" His subtext told me the question he really wanted answered.

"You do not need to pierce your dick for me, Justin Caleb Bruzzo."

His shoulders relaxed. "I'd do it, you know. For you."

"I know you would. That's sweet. But don't. Please don't. I like your cock exactly the way it is."

"Thank you. That's appreciated."

"I can imagine. There was that woman who had weights hanging from her nipple piercings, and I had to look away." I shivered, remembering.

"Did you see the one who was acting like a baby?"

"I saw the guy who was a dog, but not a baby. What room were they in?"

"The first. This was two women. The one, who couldn't have been much older than twenty-one, she had stringy maroon hair and that tattoo of Natalie Portman?"

I shook my head. She didn't sound at all familiar.

"She wore a diaper-like thing and a bib with a pacifier pinned to it. She kept making these little baby crying sounds so the other woman breastfed her."

How the hell had I missed that? "I'm glad I didn't see it. I fed Braden right before we left, but I can't even watch commercials with babies in them without feeling let down." The idea alone had me checking my breasts for leakage. "It probably wasn't a good idea to go bra-less."

JC usually never missed an opportunity to look or comment on my breasts, but he let this one pass, obviously still thinking about the party. "Did you see the woman who was flogging the guy on the St. Andrew's cross? She had all those red welts on her back and thighs. Some of them were even bleeding."

"Is that what the X cross is called?" I waited for him to nod. "I bet she'd been strapped on before we came in. They must have just switched places."

"Must have."

"I understand pain being pleasurable. I like some of that stuff, too." Like pinching and biting and hard spanking and being handled roughly. Nothing that caused bleeding. "I just think I'm not into real sadomasochism."

"Pain isn't really my thing, either."

I'd never thought it was, but it was nice to confirm that we felt the same about it. I'd never thought pain or submission would be my older sister's thing either, and yet she'd ended up married to her assistant, who was apparently a Dom in the bedroom. I'd only found out because I'd walked in on them fooling around once at her office. It was still strange to think of Norma tied to her bed or crawling on all fours, which was why I tried not to think about it at all.

JC got quiet again, thinking. "That last scene..." He trailed off, staring again out the front window.

"I know, right?" I didn't really know, though, because he still hadn't given enough clues for me to figure out how he felt about it.

To be fair, I hadn't given him much either.

I ventured to say more. "When I told Alayna I thought the party would be like watching live porn, I'd thought it would be the normal homemade sex tape variety. I had no idea it would be the hardcore black market type."

His head nodded once. "It was so…*real*."

"Brutal."

"I felt uncomfortable watching it. Aren't we supposed to be fighting against rape culture? I mean, to each his own, and I know that it was actually consensual, but I don't know."

"Yeah." Then he'd been turned off. Which was the right reaction to have. Surely. Probably.

I'd felt that way too.

I'd just felt other things as well.

I turned my head to look out the window, biting my tongue. He didn't need to know about my sick impulses of desire.

Except, wasn't the whole idea of going to The Open Door supposed to be to grow together? To open up to each other? To reconnect? How could we do that authentically if I held back my true reactions?

Taking a deep breath, I turned back to face his profile, determined to be brave. "It was disarming, yes. But I kind of thought it was hot too."

His head snapped in my direction. He studied me for seconds that seemed to stretch. "When she clawed at him?" he said finally. "That was really good. Really…hot."

I searched his eyes, looking to see if he was just telling me what he thought I wanted to hear. Everything I saw told me he was genuine.

My body twisted toward him, my pulse picking up. "And when he first grabbed her, and she was surprised. That was intense."

"I liked how she kept saying no. But you knew she really wanted it. Even though she really sounded like she meant no."

"And when he told her she deserved it." The thrill I'd felt when it had happened returned with a rush. "Hot."

"Then she clamped her thighs shut, but he forced his knee between her legs." His voice was thick, his eyes hooded.

"When he ripped her dress."

"When he put his hand at her throat."

My breath caught, imagining JC forcing his knee between *my* legs, ripping *my* dress, his hands covering *my* throat.

We held each other's gaze for a long beat, the atmosphere around us charged and pulsing. I was acutely aware of the dampness of my panties, of the shallowness of my breaths, of the hum of lust vibrating under my skin.

JC's heated expression said he was feeling much the same.

At exactly the same moment, he pulled the lever to push his seat away from the steering wheel while I climbed over the console to straddle him. Our mouths met with a crash, his tongue sweeping between my lips without hesitation. His kiss was greedy and urgent and reckless, his teeth clacking against mine as he tried to devour me. Like he couldn't get enough of me. Like he never wanted to stop. Like he couldn't if he tried.

I weaved my fingers in his hair, my nails scratching along his scalp while his hands moved behind my neck to undo the knot of my dress. As soon as it fell, his palms were on my breasts, pinching at my nipples. "All those tits everywhere, and all I wanted was to touch these." He bent his head to lick a bead of milk that had surfaced at my tip. "You have the prettiest tits I've ever seen."

I gasped as his teeth grazed along my sensitive nipple, throwing my chest up to encourage him to do it again. He did better than that, giving ample attention to both breasts with his mouth and hands, licking up the drops of milk as they leaked, triggering that build of tension in my lower belly that I loved so very much.

Without consciously being aware of my actions, my hips bucked against him. My pussy found the thick ridge of his cock pressing at the seam of his pants and began to throb. I did it again, needing more, but it wasn't enough. I reached to work his buckle, impatiently fumbling until I'd gotten his fly down. His cock fell out, heavy and hard.

"You didn't wear underwear?" I wasn't complaining.

"I didn't know what to expect tonight. I wanted to be prepared for any—fuck!" He cut off with a curse as I rubbed my pussy along his bare length. "God, you're so wet. I can feel you through your panties."

I swept my hips up again and back, whimpering with each swipe. My panties needed to be off. He needed to be inside me. But I didn't want to stop grinding long enough to make any of that possible.

He seemed just as reluctant to disconnect. His hips bucked up to meet my strokes while his mouth once again sought mine to kiss. With his lips successfully locked on mine, his fingers groped under my skirt for my clit.

"No, no. Inside," I panted. "I need you inside." My clit was getting enough friction with me sitting on top of him. He didn't need to bother with that. He needed to address my desperate need to be filled.

In an attempt to help out, I reached between my thighs and pushed the crotch panel aside. It was a tight pair of panties though, without much slack in the material, which made the task of providing room for him particularly hard.

I growled in frustration, unenthusiastic about climbing off him long enough to strip the stupid things off of me.

"Hold on," JC said just as I'd begun to lift myself out of his lap. "Let me…"

His words trailed away as he gripped the lace in both of his hands and pulled them in opposite directions. After a tense few seconds of nothing happening, the material began to tear apart. The elastic bands seemed tougher to break through. He abandoned the attempt immediately and concentrated on just getting enough fabric pulled away to give him room.

"That's harder than it looks," he said as he positioned his cock at my now bare entrance.

"That was hot," I corrected before sliding down the length of him with a gasp of relief. When I was fully seated, my insides stretching from his size, I lingered just long enough to feel him, to *really* feel him—feel how he filled me, how he pulsed hot and hard against my walls, how his crown sat deep in the center of me.

It was only a second, two at most, and then I rode.

I rode him wild, like I hadn't in who knew how long. My hands clutched his shoulders to steady myself. With swift, frantic beats of my thighs, my hips circled this way than that, eliciting the most sensual sounds from his throat. I echoed him with breathy pants as each stroke hit my clit in exactly the right way, and the sweet storm gathered inside me.

"You're such a dirty girl," my husband said, kissing my breasts as he plumped them with his hands. "So fucking dirty. Grinding on me with your pussy like that. When did you get so filthy, huh? So fucking depraved."

His words spurred me on, drove me to ride harder and faster, despite my screaming thigh muscles. I was going to feel this in the morning, and I didn't care one bit. Filthy girls didn't give attention to discomfort. Filthy girls fucked like nothing else mattered. Filthy girls fucked like they wanted to be fucked.

And I was such a dirty, filthy girl. In that moment, it was the label

I'd been longing for all my life, and I meant to earn it.

"So beautifully filthy. Such a greedy little cunt. Making a mess on my cock." JC continued to chant his disparaging praise, each new sentiment winding the tension tighter inside of me until I was at the edge of orgasm. Until I was completely there, the release exploding through me with shocking power.

My grinding came to a halt and my pussy gripped down on his cock as my body convulsed violently from the pleasure. Not missing a beat, he dug his fingers into my hips and bucked into me with rapid strokes, bringing him to his own climax while I was still recovering from mine.

"That was incredible," I said when I could speak again. I wasn't going to be able to walk for a day or two, but damn. It had been the best sex we'd had in years.

"Fan-fucking-tastic," he agreed. "See? We don't need that crazy club. We do just fine on our own."

"Yes, indeed."

With that, it seemed we'd both agreed our little outing had been a one-time adventure. The Open Door may have provided much needed inspiration to arouse our love life, but it was clear that neither of us believed it deserved enough credit to bear repeating.

Chapter Seven

Things changed between us after that.

They were subtle changes, but noticeable all the same. JC would catch me in the kitchen, heating up cereal for the baby, and he'd grab my ass. Then, instead of scowling at him or giving him a lecture about it being the wrong time—the way I'd usually react—I'd give him a flirty smile in return.

Or he'd text me something vulgar while I was working late at The Sky Launch, something he'd stopped doing ages ago. Things like:

I want to slowly spread your legs wide and bite up the inside of your thighs.

and

I've been so hard thinking about you I had to whack off into your dirty panties.

One night he didn't just text, but he showed up himself, which led to a heavy makeout session in the coat room. It was rarely used in the summer months, and all I could think was why hadn't we done this sooner?

Then came the secret Pinterest board. I got the email saying he'd shared it with me one afternoon while he was out of town. I followed the link and found a page with pictures he'd pinned, dirty pictures. Erotic pictures. Beautiful pictures of men and women in sexy poses and positions.

"*I want to do this to you,*" he had commented under a picture of a woman bent over a suited man's knee.

"*Heaven*," he'd said on another photo with a man and woman cuddling in their underwear in bed.

One of my favorite gifs was of a near naked woman sitting on a couch and a man's arm reaching from behind her to stick his hand inside her panties. "*My favorite*," JC had commented.

I started adding images too. Inspirational images. Arousing images. Images of women I thought he'd like the look of and women doing things I wanted to do to him. Images of men doing things I wanted him to do to me. Then there were the pictures of myself, sexy pictures that he later told me were his favorite on the board.

I did other things.

I'd leave the bathroom door open while I took a shower, or I'd stuff a pair of panties in his briefcase.

One afternoon while the kids napped and JC was on a business call, I walked around and "dusted" while wearing lingerie and heels. Not that the room needed dusting since the housekeepers had just been there that morning.

Obviously cleaning wasn't the point.

We flirted and touched and gazed and stared, and, while we didn't have more sex than usual, the sex we did have got significantly better. I couldn't decide if it was because of all the build-up or if we were simply more present in our moments together. Probably a little of both.

Whatever it was, I liked it. It made every ordinary day a little less mundane. More exciting. Made me remember all the reasons I'd fallen in love with him in the first place.

But the weeks went by. They turned into months, and life, as it has a tendency to do, got in the way of these simple acts. Work got busy for both of us. JC was out of town more. Jacob started kindergarten and that was a Thing that took my attention. I weaned Braden and between his crying and my aching breasts, the last thing I felt was sexy. More often than not, I'd be asleep when JC got to the bedroom at night. Or he'd be asleep when I got there. Or both of us would be tired, and, after a goodnight kiss, we'd curl up in opposite directions and pass out.

By the time September had kicked into full gear, we'd returned completely to our normal patterns, which was fine. It wasn't like we'd been unhappy before. We'd been good. Well, good enough.

Then one night around the middle of the month, I walked exhausted into the bathroom to get ready for bed and found JC had drawn me a bubble bath. I had been so eager for my head to hit the pillow I almost asked for a raincheck.

But the candles were lit and the floral scented steam rising from the tub was enticing. Besides, he'd already started stripping me from my clothes.

"Only if you're joining me," I said, letting him peel my T-shirt off my body.

"Totally planning on it."

I was glad I'd indulged as soon as I was in the water, seated between JC's legs, my back pressed up against his chest. He cleaned me thoroughly, with rapt attention, scrubbing my entire body with a natural sea sponge and my favorite body wash.

"We should take some time for ourselves." He lifted my hair to wash the back of my neck. "I've been missing you."

My first reaction was *how the hell are we supposed to do that*? I could see our calendar vividly in my head, and it was packed full.

But our anniversary was coming up, and that bore celebrating. "We could probably manage a night away. Maybe get a hotel uptown. Or Hudson and Alayna have their cabin in the Poconos. I bet they'd let us borrow it."

"That could be nice." He splashed water over my shoulders, rinsing off the soap lingering there, then bent down to kiss a spot just behind my ear. "Though I actually had something else in mind."

I couldn't see his face with him behind me, but there was hesitation in his tone, so slight I almost didn't notice it.

"Lay it on me," I said, curious now but ready to be annoyed.

He set the sponge down and wrapped his arms around me, just under my breasts. "Well, I was thinking…" He paused to nibble at my lobe. "What if we go back to The Open Door?"

My pulse quickened at the suggestion and muscles that had been relaxed just a second ago tensed up.

Always aware of my body cues, JC was quick to reassure me. "We don't have to. It's just an idea."

"I know." What I didn't know was why he'd want to go back. It had been a fun experience. Eye-opening, for sure. It had definitely given me some excellent stories to share with Alayna and my sister.

Of course when I'd told Norma the more shocking parts of the evening, hoping for some perspective on kinks I didn't understand, she'd only wanted details so she could tell her husband. Kink was such an intricate part of her life, and she was a big executive at a major company plus married with two kids. She seemed to be comfortable living her life her way.

So why did the thought of going again give me pause?

JC was quiet while I considered, letting the idea settle in, exploring my hesitancy surrounding it. There hadn't been anything there for us was my first reaction. But that hadn't been true. We'd found plenty of things that had aroused us. Aroused us enough to fuck like mad right there in our car. It had also carried into our life for weeks after. Carried in a very good way.

Did that mean we needed it now? Were we only able to get to that height of excitement with help? Did it matter if the answer was yes? We sometimes used toys at home. Wasn't a party just another useful prop?

I turned in JC's arms and fingered the dates tattooed in four lines on his left forearm. **December 19th. March 7th. January 27th. November 18th.** He hadn't had any of them when I'd met him. He'd only had one on his opposite arm, the date his former fiancée had died. The day, he'd told me, he'd died too.

Then he'd met me.

And he'd tattooed that date on his skin and told me it was the day he'd started to live again. As our boys were born, he'd added their birthdates as well, saying they were as much his reason to live now as I was.

This was my foundation as well. The five of us. The family we'd made, and the love that we shared. It was sturdy and strong and nothing was going to change that. Whether we used sex parties to make our lovemaking more thrilling or not, what we had at the base was what mattered, and it was solid.

With that understanding firm in my mind, I thought about our night at The Open Door. It had been astonishing, but it had also been fun. It had been exhilarating. It had been arousing. Even without everything that had happened once we'd walked out.

I twisted to look at my husband and brought my hand up to the back of his neck so I could pull his mouth closer to mine.

"I think that sounds like an amazing idea," I said, my lips grazing his. "How soon can we go?"

Chapter Eight

Going to The Open Door was a much different experience as a second-timer than it was as a newbie. There was less trepidation, more excitement. I didn't spend the ride worrying about my clothing—I'd chosen a leopard printed silk midi dress that was easy to move in—or my makeup, which I'd done before we left.

Instead, I imagined all the possible scenarios we'd encounter this time. Would there be another scene acted out? Another toy room? Maybe there'd be games—naughty, erotic games that involved intimately touching strangers. Or perhaps there'd be body painting. Or something crazy and weird like naked karaoke.

I was sure every idea I came up with would pale in comparison to the real thing, even though I was much better at fantasizing now. The one thing I'd definitely gotten as a result of our first go-around was inspiration. I'd never realized that struggling could be such a turn-on. Or how much I enjoyed voyeurism. The things I'd witnessed had been planted inside my mind like seeds, and now they'd sprouted into a garden of debauchery that I'd never been able to imagine before we went.

Once again, the party location for this particular Saturday was outside of Manhattan. Way outside. Two hours away in Darien, Connecticut. The trip had sounded so daunting, we'd almost selected to go another weekend. But the website indicated this event was a club annual highlight, and that was too intriguing to pass up.

There was no parking away from the house this time. The residence was located more than a mile down a private drive. As instructed beforehand, we provided a code word to the guard at the gate—*lubricious*—and were only let through once we did. Even in the dark, I had a feeling the grounds were spectacular. Trees lined both sides of the twisting road, and when I rolled down my window, I could hear the crash of ocean waves nearby.

I'd thought I'd prepared myself for the grandeur of the house at the end of the drive, but the air was knocked from my lungs when it came into view. House wasn't even the right word for it. It was a modern interpretation of a waterfront grand estate situated on the Long Island Sound. One of those country residences I'd only seen the likes of on the big screen. I'd definitely never been anywhere so luxurious.

"The house I grew up in looked a lot like this," JC said as he helped me from the car.

My jaw fell slack. I'd known he'd come from wealth, but his parents had died a long time ago, and there had never been a family for me to meet, let alone a family house to visit. "We've been married how long, and I'm just learning this now?"

He shrugged. "I guess it never came up."

Almost eight years together, and he still could surprise me. I loved that about him.

We were greeted with the same sort of check-in process as we had on our previous visit, but this time we could also hand over keys and purses and our items were locked into a large safe, and, instead of a choice of colored bracelets, we were given a string of beads to wear wherever we chose. Like the last time, we chose white, which meant no one could touch us or give us physical compliments unless we instigated it.

We'd just finished adorning our beads—I'd put mine around my neck while JC had chosen to wrap it around his wrist—we were approached by a gorgeous masked woman wearing a Victorian gothic white and red dress.

"First time?" she asked.

JC and I exchanged glances. We'd managed to keep to ourselves at the last party. We hadn't tried to engage with anyone, and, for the most part, no one had tried to talk to us. I'd liked the ability to be cocooned in our own adventure. But perhaps we would have gotten more out of the whole thing if we hadn't been so reclusive.

JC must have come to the same conclusion, only faster than I did because he answered first. "Second time. Is it that obvious?"

She laughed. "Not necessarily. I'm just what's known as a frequent flyer, and I didn't recognize your faces. Glad to have you both. I'm Miss T."

JC opened his mouth, presumably to give our own names, when I interrupted. "Should we have code names? Is that a thing people do at these things?"

Again she laughed. It wasn't a patronizing sound, but a light, friendly tinkle. "Not at all. It's one of my personal rules. There are others who prefer not to use names here, just as there are people who never take off their masks—I'm one of those, too. I see too many of these people at the office, and I don't think my boss would be too happy knowing what his clients are doing with his secretary on the weekends. It's much better that none of them recognize me. But there are just as many people who are happy to share everything. And I mean *everything*."

"Ah," I said, imagining circumstances where I might feel the same. Since we were really only here to watch, it didn't seem like a big issue for us. And JC was already known for showing his fellow investors a good time as part of business procedure. "Then I'm Gwen." I looked to my spouse for permission before adding, "And this is my husband, JC."

"Good to meet you, and welcome! Have you been out back yet? Would you like me to take you to the grounds?"

"Out back?" Once again, JC and I exchanged a glance. "Is the party outside?"

"It is! This estate is one of the few locations that is private enough to allow frolicking outdoors. It's the only reason most everyone would drive all the way out here, including me."

"Then frolicking outdoors is a major draw?" Maybe I needed to frolic more to understand.

She seemed about to answer, then changed her mind. "I think it will be easier to show you. Come on. I'll take you."

With a shrug, I took my husband's hand and followed after our mysterious new friend.

"The two parties we've been to now have been outside of New York," JC commented as T led us through a nearly empty sitting room. "Is that common?"

"In the summer, more often than not, the club moves out to the surrounding suburbs. Most people are glad to escape the city heat. After tonight, though, the events mainly take place in Manhattan."

It seemed like a waste not to take advantage of T's knowledge so I asked my own question. "The check-in was different too. Last time we were given bracelets. Are the beads new?"

"Those vary per the host," T explained. "All depends on who's in charge, so make sure to always carefully read the instructions for entrance on the website. Sometimes there's a code word to get in, sometimes there are bracelets, sometimes there's glow-in-the-dark body paint. Personally, I like necklaces best, because then you can leave them on a door handle if you decide to use a room. Lets others know if you want anyone to join you or not."

People just walk in and join strangers who are already having sex?

My face went red as I thought about it. I didn't know why that was any different than half of the stuff we'd already seen. I'd just figured that the guests who used the rooms were specifically looking for privacy and had already chosen who they wanted to be messing around with.

JC must have been equally surprised by the notion because he gave my hand a solidarity squeeze.

"I should let you know, too, that most of the events aren't this extravagant. They're all different in their own ways, but this one is something special." T took us around a corner, and now we were in a great room with large windows overlooking the landscape. The ocean stretched across the background like thick black ink, but the grounds were completely lit up, and the reason this particular party was special became clearly evident.

Because it wasn't just a party—it was a full-blown festival.

The yard was completely filled with people—dressed-up people, skimpily dressed people, people wearing masks, people wearing couture, people wearing outrageous costumes and plumes, people wearing nothing at all—more people than had been in all the rooms combined at the last event. Some lounged on the grass or in deck chairs, fooling around like they had at the first party, but most of them were clustered around various areas of activity, like they did at a circus or a carnival. What those activities were, exactly, was difficult to discern from where we stood.

"Whoa," JC said, staring wide-eyed at the scene in front of us.

"Whoa," I echoed, not knowing where to look first.

"Come on outside. You can't tell what's going on from here." T had apparently continued walking without us and now beckoned to us from an open set of French doors.

"I'll let you explore on your own," she said when we were all outside. "But if you need anything, please come and find me. I know the club can be a bit overwhelming to newbies, especially on a night like tonight. I assure you, though, there's something for everyone."

With so much going on around us, I could believe it. Now to figure out what the party had for us.

"To the right then?" JC asked after we'd thanked Miss T for her guidance.

"It seems as good a place to start as any."

We headed past a small clump of guests making out on the lawn to the first group gathered to the right of us and found a trio of artists. One of them drew art with henna on guests' bodies—anywhere the guest wanted it. Another painted kinky drawings on people's backs. The last one was a sketch artist, the kind found at any state fair who would quickly pencil portraits, the only difference was that this one drew his subjects naked.

"I'm not comfortable taking off my clothes," I said when he offered to draw me.

"You don't have to take off anything," he said, reassuringly. "If you stay dressed, I simply have to use my imagination."

I was sure that wasn't something JC would go for—another man openly picturing his wife naked—but when I looked to him, he surprised me. "Go ahead. I'd love to see this."

I sat down in the provided chair, nervous to see what the artist came up with. "But what if he draws me better than I look?"

"Impossible," JC said, amazing husband that he was.

He was wrong, in the end, because the Gwen that was in the sketch that I was handed twenty minutes later had a decidedly flatter stomach and firmer thighs.

"I have better boobs," I said. "Or I did. They've sort of deflated since I stopped nursing."

JC studied the portrait. "Nah. You still have better boobs."

We continued around the yard from there, finding a myriad of sinful distractions and erotic pleasures. One area had vibrating saddles like we'd seen at the party before—Sybians, I learned they were called. After that was a naked limbo competition and the human carousel where people rode other people rather than painted horses. We skipped the Tent of Torture, but everyone who walked out seemed more than a little bit happy about whatever they'd seen inside. We saw another fire massage then watched an erotic massage that was basically the same as a regular massage except the masseuse didn't shy away from the woman's tits or ass, and in the end she fingered her to orgasm.

There was also a bunch of things that could be found at most festivals. There was a juggler and a man on stilts and a knife thrower. There was a variety of clowns, some with their outfit painted on, some with no outfit at all. The contortionist was also naked, which was more awkward to watch than sensual. The bouncy house looked fun, but I'd gone braless and the idea of jumping around without one just made my boobs hurt. I did appreciate the very large belly dancer who was amazingly flexible and could shake her hips faster than Shakira.

Then there were the games—Twister, Spin the Bottle, Strip Jenga. There was a game where people had to pass a dildo from person to person without using their hands and another game where they had to put a condom on a long balloon only using their mouth. We watched for a while, cheering one couple on in the balloon game until they were named the champions.

After that, we wandered over to watch the acrobats on the tightrope that had been erected over the pool. Some of the spectators watched from the water itself, others from the lawn, still more from lounge chairs. As many of the people gathered were distracted with their own erotic gymnastics as they were in watching, which added to the entertainment. We enjoyed that for quite a while before tiring of it.

We'd practically made it around the whole yard when we got to the kissing booths. One was manned by a young, gorgeous Latina brunette with large eyes and plump lips. She was dressed, though barely, with her petite breasts exposed to the nipple. The other booth featured an equally beautiful man with dark chocolate skin and a sexy bald head that I itched to rub my hands over.

"Your turn," I told JC, nudging him toward the female. "Kiss her."

"Uh, yeah. I don't think so. Our rules were no sharing, no touching—"

"I know what the rules were. This is different. It's a kissing booth." Not that I had any misconceptions that the kissing that happened here would be as tame as any other kissing booth I'd encountered. But I knew it would stop there, and, in the safety of this environment, I wondered what JC looked like kissing another woman. I wanted to watch it.

He was hesitant. "Are you sure?"

"Very. Besides, she's hot. *I'd* kiss her."

"Okay, I'll do it. But only if you do it too."

I glanced over at the other booth where the beautiful man was currently tonguing a man old enough to be his grandpa.

"Not him," JC said, obviously not as comfortable with watching his wife kiss another man as I was with him kissing another woman. "I meant only if you kiss *her.*"

Goosebumps ran down my arms. I'd never kissed another girl before. I wasn't exactly against it, I'd just never had any interest. Or maybe never had the opportunity.

But now, the idea of kissing this gorgeous woman, particularly right after she'd kissed my husband, particularly knowing my husband was getting off on our kissing, made me wet between the legs.

"Sure," I agreed.

JC stepped up to the booth, and I scurried to his side where I could have an up-close view. The woman—almost a girl, she was so young—initiated the act, reaching behind his neck to pull my husband down to her mouth. She was somewhat aggressive, kissing with more confidence and prowess than I'd ever had. Her mouth was open from the very beginning, and I could see when her tongue slipped in between his lips.

I studied them with interest, trying to decide if I was at all jealous. I focused on the worst about the situation in my head, too, just to really test the idea. *She's younger than you,* I told myself. *Her boobs don't sag even a little bit. I bet she's more adventurous in bed. JC would probably love that.*

Even though JC kissed her back, even though I caught a glimpse of his tongue coming out to meet hers, the only emotion I could identify feeling was curiosity. It didn't mean anything. *She* didn't mean anything, and he proved it by being the one to pull away first.

"Do you always kiss with your eyes open?" I asked when he looked over at me as if to gauge my reaction.

"Not always. When I don't know the person, I guess."

"Huh." It seemed like an odd answer, for some reason, but not a bothersome one. I definitely didn't close my eyes when it was my turn, and her soft, swollen lips wrapped around mine. She was a good kisser. She tasted like cinnamon and cigarettes and, faintly, I swore I could taste JC on her tongue, which made my skin buzz. My belly tightened thinking of him, and I could feel the urge to whimper at the back of my throat as she worshipped my mouth.

The whole time, what I really wanted to know was what JC thought about it.

He seemed to want to know the same. "Well?" he said the second we were finished.

I laughed and thanked the young woman before taking his hand and tugging him away from the booth.

"Well?" he asked again, adjusting the bulge in his pants, which told me exactly what he'd thought about it.

"It was nice," I admitted. "She was a really good kisser."

We found a bench in a quiet spot on the patio, and we sat to watch a pair of sensual dancers who'd just begun performing on the lawn. Their performance was gorgeous and fascinating to watch, but I was distracted by what had happened right before. I still wasn't really bothered by JC kissing the stranger, which I considered a healthy response.

I was intrigued, however, with his reaction to her kissing *me*.

What did that mean about him? Did he secretly want to watch me with another woman? Did he fantasize about a threesome? And how did I feel about that if he did?

It was hot, in theory. I liked an attractive woman, and while I had no desire to go down on one, I would probably enjoy one going down on me.

But another woman going down on JC was a whole different situation. Even if I was there too, it felt like a big deal. Felt like crossing a line. A line that I wasn't sure that a couple could ever come back from.

It wasn't something I needed to worry about. JC hadn't ever suggested he wanted a threesome. And there were a lot of things that were hot to fantasize about that I never wanted to actually do. We didn't have to do that. I knew that. I truly did.

Then why couldn't I get the idea of it out of my mind?

Chapter Nine

While I was lost in my thoughts, the performance of the sensual dancers evolved, and, when I bothered to look up again, the pair had been joined by another male. The trio swept across the lawn with sultry movements and spectacular lifts, then coming together to embrace before parting again. The dance gave a vivid impression of a courtship—the highs, the lows, the chase.

I glanced at JC and found him rapt. I turned back to the dancers. They were beautiful and talented, but they didn't enthrall me the way they'd enthralled my husband.

In fact, nothing at the party had captured my attention in that way. Not in the way I wanted to be captured. The carnal carnival, overall, was erotic and bawdy and captivating, and I'd enjoyed myself completely. But I wasn't aroused like so many others around us. There might have been a moment or two where I'd felt a spike of want, but nothing had me itching in my skin with desire. Nothing had me desperate for the next level. Nothing tantalized me to the point of needing to touch and be touched.

Though, I'd learned that, for myself, the touching was often what led to the yearning. Maybe I needed to be cuddling more with JC.

Honestly, I didn't know what I expected or wanted, even. We'd come to have time together and find inspiration to inject some sexiness into our day-to-day life, and I'd definitely been inspired. It had never been the intention to actually participate in anything while there.

Just, with all the free love happening around us, I wondered if I was somehow missing out.

Or, more accurately, I wondered if JC was missing out, and what I should do about it if he was.

A wave of laughter drew my attention to a group of partiers nearby who appeared to be playing some sort of strip game of truth or dare. Clothes were shed at each round. The heavy air of lust clung everywhere around them—I could feel it even from where I sat.

One of the players was Miss T, who'd lost her dress now and was only wearing a white lace corset and frilly panties. When she saw me watching, she stepped out of the circle and waved me over.

I patted JC's arm. "I'll be right back." I stood and crossed over to our new friend.

"Enjoying yourself?" T asked when I reached her.

I nodded but paused before answering. "Yeah. I mean, yes. I'm having a good time."

"You sound like you're either trying to convince me or you're trying to convince yourself. And, honey, you don't need to put on a front for me, if that's what you're doing. If this isn't your jam, it's not your jam."

"No, it's my jam," I said quickly. For whatever reason, I was defensive.

I thought for a second about how to say what I was feeling. "It's all very fascinating and exciting and it interests me very much, so much that I want to take it to the next level. But I can't figure out how to participate when both JC and I are committed to only being with each other. Maybe this place is more suited to singles and swingers."

"I don't think that's true. It might not end up being suited for you and JC, but there are a lot of couples that come here that aren't swapping. I'm not exactly married, but practically. We both attend nearly every week, and we've never fucked anyone but each other. There isn't a one-size fits all about what people want from The Open Door. That's why there are three different colors of beads."

"You're in a relationship?" I hadn't realized since I'd only seen her by herself, and the beads she wore were red, the color that invited people to touch and compliment without verbal consent. "If you don't mind me asking, what does that look like for the two of you? Do you have rules? How far do you go with other people?" I hadn't minded JC's kiss at the kissing booth, but I didn't want him kissing in other scenarios, especially if those scenarios could lead beyond kissing. And I sure as hell didn't want him touching other women.

So what did that leave?

"Oh, everyone has rules," she said. "Most everyone. Not just couples, either. I never slept with anyone even before I was with Nate. And I have the mask and the name, but others have their own guidelines. Whatever they need to make it feel safe for them, you know?"

I nodded. JC and I had made the rules not to share and not to touch, and both of us had abided by them, easily. I loved the idea of doing things our way, but we'd needed—well, I'd needed—to define what that was in order to feel comfortable here.

"As for Nate and me"—T gestured to a fully clothed man in a suit sitting just beyond where the game was taking place, a man I assumed was the Nate she spoke of—"I don't mind you asking, but I can tell you right now that how we work isn't how everyone works. Myself, I love touching. I come here to touch other people and to have people touch me. Nate, on the other hand, loves watching. I've never asked him not to engage with anyone, but he usually doesn't anyway. It's just not his thing. He's never asked me not to engage either, because, first of all, we'd be over if he did, and secondly, he genuinely likes watching me fool around.

"I know some other couples here that have different boundaries, too. Liz and Steve have a kissing only rule and Sheri and Melissa allow anything as long as their clothes stay on. Kayti is a Domme, and she'll play with different subs, give them head sometimes, but they can never touch her back. Eric and Troy have a rule that they both have to be involved. Who else….? Oh, Jill and Ben will participate in games, but nothing else. And a ton of people come here just to watch then go home. Or they go upstairs, find a room, and bang loud enough for everyone else to hear. Like I said, it's a personal decision. Talk with your husband, and you'll find what works for both of you, and if it's only watching, that's still participating. Believe me, it's all welcome."

I sighed, feeling a bit ridiculous and a lot naïve. "You're right. I'm worrying too much about it. Thank you for saying what I needed to hear."

She went back to her game, and I went back to JC, less concerned about what everyone else was doing, more focused on what my husband and I wanted out of the experience. He was standing now, and I couldn't help but notice the crotch of his pants was bulging.

Watching was apparently enough for him.

It would be enough for me too.

I sat next to him and stroked the back of his leg with my palm to let him know I'd returned. He smiled down at me then gave his attention back to the performance, dropping his hand to rub affectionately at the back of my neck.

With his fingers playing at my nape, I focused on the show as well. The dancers, who'd stripped their clothes while I was gone, still moved with deliberate and performative movements, and now they were also in what appeared to be the late stages of foreplay. Both men's cocks were hard, and the woman was inches away from putting one of them inside her.

Okay, now that was hot.

Really hot.

My nipples were sharp points as she glided down on the man beneath her, then up again, then down, all in time to the music. And when the second man pushed her down so he could shove inside her ass, my panties were flooded.

Damn, it was erotic. It was gorgeously choreographed and yet the dancers were still very authentically fucking. It was like watching an artsy porn, and who wouldn't get turned on by that?

People who didn't go to sex parties, maybe, but here, it seemed, lots of people felt how I felt. As I scanned the audience, I discovered most everyone was completely engrossed. Some of them were fooling around as well. Most only petting and making out, but a few had gone further, fucking along with the performers, and a woman in front of us had her hand in her panties.

Watching all the sex around me was definitely a turn on.

Except, the thing I found the most arousing, the thing that had me fidgeting and needing relief wasn't watching everyone fumble and grope and fuck, but imagining that *I* was the one being watched.

Oh, yeah. That really did it for me. Made my pussy buzz and clench.

It shouldn't have come as such a surprise. I'd always liked the idea of being watched, always liked the prospect of getting caught. As much as I'd always been into it, though, I'd never considered if I'd like the real thing and not just the fantasy. It wasn't something I'd ever had reason to consider.

Here, in a place where public screwing wasn't a criminal offense, I couldn't help but consider it. Not only consider it, but try it out.

Or maybe not.

Instantly, I was having doubts, and I hadn't even completely made up my mind. I wasn't comfortable being naked in front of strangers, and I didn't know that I could relax enough to do the deed with so many spectators, not on the first go.

I needed to take baby steps.

Before I could talk myself out of it, I angled myself toward JC and reached for his belt. He turned toward me, his body moving a beat ahead of his eyes that were still pinned to the orgy on the makeshift stage.

When he saw what I was doing, he raised one questioning eyebrow. But he didn't stop me, letting me unthread the leather from the loops and undo the buckle.

"Is this okay?" I asked, pausing at the button of his pants.

He paused, studying my face, and I had a feeling his hesitation had more to do with making certain I was okay with it than deciding that he was. Eventually, he nodded once. "If you're not sure…"

I gave my honest answer. "I'm sure."

Still, as sure as I was, my hands shook as I undid the button and brought the zipper down. I was excited. I was eager. As soon as I had his pants open, JC's cock popped out, fat and full. Like last time, he'd gone sans underwear, maybe hoping for some more car action after.

Or maybe hoping for something like this.

I licked my lips and pumped his length with my hand while I glanced around. No one was watching us…yet. But someone could at any moment.

The thought made me have to squeeze my thighs together real hard.

I stroked up and down him a few times, my palm caressing his crown each time I reached the top. He was completely ready. He was so hard that he throbbed in my hand. He was going to go quick if I let him.

With my eyes lifted toward the man I loved, I lowered my mouth to his tip and gave it a swipe with my tongue.

His exhale was audible.

I licked him a few more times, teasing him before taking his head between my lips. The familiar taste of him and the reality of what I was doing, of where I was doing it, made me moan. His entire body shuddered from the vibration, and he made a low rumble in the back of his throat.

The sound made me squirm. I wanted him to do it again.

Fisting him with one hand, I drew him into my mouth, bobbing rhythmically while I silently counted to five. Then I flattened my tongue and ran it across his crown, delighting in the bead of pre-cum that waited there. I quickly licked it up then repeated my sequence—fisting, bobbing, swipe of my tongue at the top, repeat.

After I'd taunted him like this for a while, he took my hair in both hands. I expected he meant to take over, to hurry things along, but he just tugged at the strands, the bite of pain making me shiver.

"You're such a tease." His voice was raw, his eyes clouded. His head turned to survey our surroundings. "People are watching."

I felt a gush between my legs. I wanted to stop and look myself, wanted to ask him how many people and what their reactions were, but I also didn't want to break the spell.

Besides, JC knew what I needed. "Several people. They can't help it. You're too beautiful sucking cock for them to look away. There's a man across the patio whose eyes are glued on you. He's got his cock out too. You've made him hard, Gwen. Watching you has made him hard."

His words came out ragged, and they made me crazed. Made me greedier and more eager to please him. I abandoned the tormenting and proceeded enthusiastically, jacking him with one hand as I sucked his crest with my mouth. I tilted my head this way and that to vary the strokes, to draw him deeper on some and more shallow on others.

Maybe I wasn't completely done taunting him after all.

His patience had worn off, however. He moved his hands to cradle my head, holding it still so he could fuck it how he wanted. At his own speed. Thrusting his hips with a primal frenzy that took my arousal to the next level.

And people were watching!

I imagined the way we must look, my eyes watering, my cheeks hollowed, and my husband's big cock greedily fucking my mouth. Low in my stomach, the beginnings of an orgasm stirred. I'd never come from giving pleasure, and I probably wouldn't now, but holy shit, it wasn't an impossibility.

"Fuck, Gwen." JC's grip tightened on my head, and I could feel his body tense, the one tell he was there before I felt the spurt of cum shoot across my tongue. Still, he didn't slow down, and I struggled to swallow as he thrust on, bucking his hips against my face, the tip of his cock touching the back of my throat with every stroke.

Then his entire body convulsed and another gush filled my mouth.

I took it all, swallowing every last drop.

He still wasn't completely soft when he pulled me to my feet to kiss him. I wondered if he could taste himself in my mouth as his tongue licked between my lips.

"You are fucking incredible. You know that?"

I giggled and let him kiss me again, his face cool against my hot skin. I felt flushed from what I'd done, from his compliment, and when I remembered we had an audience, my cheeks darkened further, even though I wasn't embarrassed about what we'd done. On the contrary, I felt cocky. I felt full of myself.

Did JC feel the same?

Recalling what T had said about communicating, I asked him, "Was that all right? Would you have rather I didn't—"

He cut me off. "Did you hear me say you were incredible? It was perfect, babe. *You* were perfect. I loved every minute of it."

I moaned this time as his kiss grew deeper. I was still very deeply aroused, a fact that had to be obvious to JC and anyone who was still watching by the way my body pressed against him, the way my thigh wrapped around his leg. The way my hips ground against him.

He broke away and murmured against my lips, "I want you." He glanced around, as if looking for a close place to drag me to and have his way. "I need to make you feel good too. I need to be inside you."

Was there a silent question there? Was he asking how far I wanted to take this? If I wanted to continue this publicly or was he simply eager to return the favor?

A part of me—a big part of me—wanted to keep pushing my boundaries. It would be so easy to hitch up my dress and let him fuck me against the side of the house. No one would see anything. Not really, but they'd be able to see enough to make it damn hot.

Did I want to go that far?

With great effort, I peeled myself off of him and grasped his hand in mine. "Let's go to the car," I said. "You can tell me more about what everyone was doing while I sucked you, and then you can make me feel good too."

I'd discovered something I enjoyed. Discovering it with the person I loved most in the world made it feel significantly more profound. There was no need to rush taking it to another level. I had as long as I had JC to explore this newfound kink, and I had him forever.

Chapter Ten

We had sex for eight days straight after that. The only reason it wasn't longer was that JC had to go out of town, and, if the extreme amounts of sexting counted as sex, then our running streak was more like two weeks.

Discovering the power that being watched had on my libido stimulated our love life in ways I'd never imagined. Memories of the night itself got me revved up every time I thought about it. When their potency began to diminish, fantasizing and role playing similar situations worked just as well.

And it wasn't just me—both of us had gotten off on it.

"It makes me feel like the most envied man in the room," JC had told me a few days later. "People get to watch, but they don't get to touch, and how can they not want to when you're as incredibly sexy as you are? It's an ego booster, for sure. It makes me feel like a rock star. It makes me feel like a god."

I'd always thought of him as a sex god. That he was finally recognizing this for himself felt validating, and it only made me want him more.

He'd fucked me hard bent over the side of the playpen then. It was empty at the time—we weren't so out-of-control that we'd become inappropriate in front of the children, but we were connected in a way that we hadn't been before. We were in synch with each other and more in love than ever. Now we were learning how to take advantage of every moment alone, even brief stolen moments in the playroom while the kids took their naps.

Even when our lovemaking slowed down to a more normal pace,

the effects carried on in other areas. Every moment of my life felt charged for the first time in years. For the first time since when I'd first met JC, and he'd taken me on an exploration of sexual freedom that I'd ever known. Instead of going through my days by rote, my mind constantly wandering to more urgent matters like employee schedules and my grocery list, I started to live more presently. I was more in my body, more aware of my senses and the people around me, particularly when one of those people was my husband. I was like a radio tuned to his signal. All he had to do was walk in a room, and the energy between us crackled and surged.

The decision to go back to The Open Door was a no-brainer. The only issue was fitting it into our busy lives. Between work and the kids and family and friend obligations, our schedule was booked for the following four weeks.

On the first Saturday in November, the stars aligned and JC and I found ourselves at a penthouse uptown for our first party in the City.

Like we had in the past, we'd walked in with guidelines. Also like in the past, I felt the need to reiterate them as soon as we'd finished checking in.

"Don't forget," I said, "We both have to agree if we do this, and I don't want anyone seeing me naked. Oh, and the same rules as before—no sharing, no touching anyone else."

"Are you really afraid I'm not going to remember?"

"No," I admitted. "I'm just nervous."

He tucked me under his arm and bent his head close to mine. "Well, I'm not nervous. I'm excited. And eager." He ran his tongue along the sensitive spot of my ear. "But I'm going to make sure it's everything you want and nothing else. Trust me."

I took a deep breath and let my body surrender into his on the exhale. "Okay."

Unlike in the past, tonight we had an agenda. Tonight we planned to fuck, not in the car, but at the party. And when we did, we sure as hell meant to be watched.

The penthouse location gave a very different vibe than when we'd been in the suburbs. There was less structure to the event. Less costume. Less pomp and spectacle. There were still organized activities, but not as many as previously. With the more lax structure and the smaller space, the guests were forced to mingle more. It was harder to find a quiet corner as we had the last time.

But I was determined.

We meandered through the front room, staying long enough for the erotic poetry reading to be polite before making our way into the interior. The den/dining room was the designated pain area, and we skipped that altogether. It was the first real cold night New York had experienced this season, but a cluster of guests had made their way to the hot tub on the terrace. As far as I could tell looking from the safety of the warm apartment, none of them had brought swimwear.

"There's a fire pit going out there," JC said, peering over my shoulder. "And the outdoor sofa is empty. I bet we'd be warm enough."

I bit my lip, considering. "I think it's a space that will attract too many people." I wanted to feel like I was being watched, but I wasn't interested in anyone thinking they could join in.

JC understood. "I get you. Let's keep going."

The kitchen and the hallway were free spaces with no particular focus. They were also unusually crowded. Even though I was wearing white beads, I was groped no less than four times trying to make it to the library. The last time, when the hand that squeezed my breast from behind accompanied warm lips at the back of my neck, JC nearly punched the guy in the face.

"My bad, my bad," the paunchy gentleman said, his hands raised up in surrender. "Didn't see the beads."

I tugged on my husband's jacket, urging him to let it go and continue down the hall with me. He came, reluctantly, but he wasn't done with the groper. "Even the red beads aren't an invitation to fondle without permission," he shouted behind us. "Consent, man! Enthusiastic consent!"

As soon as we were safely pressed against a wall of books in the two-story library, I kissed him for that. "Consent is sexy," I said, pausing to explain. "Thank you for being my knight and defending my honor."

We made out for several minutes, our hands and mouths moving frantically. I was quickly wet and aroused, and I knew I wasn't alone because his erection was pressing firmly against my hip. Would this be where we did it? I'd deliberately worn no panties and a dress that could be easily rucked up. All JC had to do was hoist me up around his waist and press me against the bookshelf behind us.

But was this the right room?

Though he didn't say it, I could tell he was wondering the same thing when he broke our kiss and scanned the room without letting go of his tight grip on my ass. I looked around as well. It was a quieter area, which I liked, but it was by no means boring. A small game of strip poker was being played around the desk. The sofa at the other end of the room hosted a cluster of cuddling guests, their feet so tangled around each other it was hard to determine what appendage belonged to whom. More people were scattered around the room in intimate groups of three or four, talking and petting and kissing.

"Look over there." JC nodded toward a trembling woman standing nearby, her hands braced on the bookshelves as her legs shook uncontrollably.

It took a few seconds to realize there was another woman eating her out under her skirt, and still another beat before I noticed the woman on the ground wasn't just sitting on a man's lap, but was being privately fucked at the same time.

"Oh." My body temperature spiked suddenly. With my eyes still on the threesome, I palmed JC's cock through his pants. "That's really hot."

"I think they're trying to be discreet. And that might be the hottest part." He nipped along my neck. "I want you, Gwen. I want to be discreet inside you right here."

"I want that too. So much."

His palm closed around one of my breasts. "That handsy douchebag thought you were his to touch. I'm not going to be able to see straight until I can remind everyone you're mine."

Possessive alpha husband mode—*yes, yes, yes.*

I nodded eagerly, making sure to give him my enthusiastic consent before he locked his mouth to mine and pivoted me so that my back hit the bookcase. I spread my legs, making room for him between them. He ground his hips back and forth against my pelvis, rubbing my clit with his expert tilt. God, he felt good. Even with the edge of the shelf pushing into my back. It was uncomfortable and would probably leave a bruise, but I was too turned on to care.

There were other elements of the room, however, that distracted me. The hoots and hollers from the strip poker group when some guy lost his last article of clothing, the cry of pleasure from one of the women in the threesome when she'd finally found her orgasm, the whispers and giggles from the heap of cuddlers. It was hard to believe anyone was watching us with all that was going on, and try as I might to concentrate on what I was doing—on what was being done to me—I couldn't help but be aware of everything else.

JC was petting the wet slit beneath my skirt when the loud smack of skin against skin pulled my attention enough to look away from my husband. A new couple had entered the room, and I could swear I knew the masked woman who was currently getting her ass spanked by her lover.

"Is that Celia?" I didn't know Alayna's husband's ex all that well so I couldn't be sure.

JC dropped my skirt to look at the blonde draped across the older man's lap. "Possibly. I think so."

He bent to kiss me again, but I pushed him away. "I can't do this if that's Celia."

"It's probably not her. I don't know her well enough."

He obviously wasn't bothered by the idea.

I definitely was.

Pulling away from him altogether, I straightened my dress and crossed my arms over my breasts. "But what if it *is* her?" I whispered harshly. It was one thing to fuck in front of an anonymous crowd, but quite a different thing to do it in front of someone we might know, no matter how distant the relation.

He adjusted himself. "Should we stop?"

"Yes." The mood had been killed now anyway.

No. That was a lie. I was still raring to go, just not in current company. "I don't know," I corrected.

"Then we should stop." He was trying to be supportive, but the flat tone of his voice suggested it wasn't easy.

With the hard-on he was sporting, I didn't have to imagine why.

I huffed in frustration. This wasn't how I'd imagined the night going, which was probably part of the problem. I'd imagined it far too often. The scenario was too firm in my mind—we'd find a visible yet away spot and, even though all eyes might not be on us, it would *feel* like they were on us.

Now that we'd seen the layout of this particular party, I was beginning to see my fantasy likely couldn't be played out to ideal. That was disappointing. And a turn-off. At this point, I wasn't sure we could get on course again at all.

Maybe we should just go and try another night.

On the other hand, JC was as ready to get it on as ever. We'd looked forward to this evening for so long. Both of us had. I didn't want to let him down, but more importantly, I didn't want to let *us* down.

Leaving now would mean both of us going home with a major case of blue balls. And I really hated having blue balls.

"I don't want to stop," I said, taking his hand in mine. "Let's just...can we look for another room? Somewhere a little less...busy?"

"Yes, hon. Anywhere you want." He laced his fingers through mine and, after a brief survey of our options, led us across the library to the spiral staircase. Single file, we climbed to the second floor. The floor with the bedrooms.

We'd never been to the bedrooms at these parties. I'd expected to find one big giant orgy, but that wasn't exactly the case. There were four bedrooms in total. The first room was occupied by two couples who weren't engaging together, perhaps two pairs of swingers who'd swapped spouses for the night. At the second room, we found a naked man blindfolded and tied to the bed. The third door was closed, but the sounds of rough sex floated clearly to those outside.

The last door we came to was open, and the bedroom empty. The weird thing was that so many people were in the hallway, which couldn't be as comfortable as the room was, even if they only wanted to talk. No one was really talking, though. They just hung out, some standing along the wall, others sitting, their backs propped up against it.

"Are any of you waiting for that room?" JC asked no one in particular.

A very curvy woman with purple hair and a tube top turned to answer him. "We're waiting for someone to put on a show, if that's what you're asking."

The Latino next to her perked up. "We've been saving it just for you," he said, waggling his brows.

JC and I exchanged glances. These people were waiting to watch, and here we were, wanting to be watched. It should have been perfect.

It still could be perfect.

I just had to figure out how I felt about being on a stage.

"We can go home," JC offered quietly. "Or we can keep looking for something else. Or we can—"

I cut him off. "Let's do it." It wasn't how I'd imagined it, but nothing ever was.

JC was entirely too patient with me sometimes. "Are you sure?"

I took the white bead necklace from my neck and hung it on the door, earning a woot from a handful of onlookers, then I kissed him hard. "How's that for enthusiastic consent?"

Laughing, he towed me into the room. "I enthusiastically consent too. Now, let's get you naked."

I barely had time to glare at him before he pulled me flush against him.

"Kidding," he whispered against my lips. "Clothes on. No one sees you naked. I know what you want."

He pressed his mouth to mine, and the things he did with his tongue made it easier to ignore the audience we had in the hall. His lips weren't the only thing pressing against me, either. His erection was back, not that I was sure it had ever gone away. I'd been too preoccupied to notice.

But now I definitely noticed.

Quickly, I undid his pants just enough to reach in and stroke him. He hadn't made the same specifications about not wanting to be seen naked, but I didn't really want everyone seeing his body. It belonged only to me. And, while I didn't get aroused like he did by flaunting my ownership, I was still possessive about what was mine.

As I continued to fondle him, he brought his hand to my breast to pinch at my nipple. "You're so turned on right now. You're so wet, I can smell your pussy."

I tried to press my thighs together to ease the ache, but JC nudged his knee between my legs, propping me open. With one hand firmly gripping the back of my neck, he brought his other hand down to finger my folds, making sure to keep my dress draped so that no one could see.

They couldn't see, but it was obvious what was happening. JC knew my body so well that I was gasping and grasping on to him short minutes later.

"Don't hold it in," he urged me. "Let everyone hear how well I treat you."

I hadn't forgotten our spectators—they were half the reason I was close to climax so fast—but his reminder of their existence accentuated their part in my lust. My orgasm doubled in on itself, and a long, low cry wrenched from my throat while my body shook and stuttered with pleasure.

I was vaguely aware of JC murmuring praise and dirty encouragement while he helped me down to the bed, as well as what might have been praise and dirty encouragement coming from the hallway, which was hot-as-fuck. After pulling my ass to the edge, he propped my feet on the mattress, my bent knee preventing any glimpse of what was happening behind it. He met my eyes as he positioned his cock at my hole.

"Do you want me?" he asked, teasing the tip inside me.

"Yes."

"That doesn't sound like you mean it." He pushed a little farther inside then quickly stroked back out. "I'm not going to give you what you don't want."

"You're such a fucking tease." I lifted my hips to try to meet him, but he pulled all the way out with a laugh. I groaned.

"Mean it," he said, taunting my clit with his head.

"Fuck me!" I begged. "Please, please, I need you to fuck me!"

I was dizzy with need, greedy and eager, yet I wasn't so mindless that I wasn't aware that this was for the audience. This was for their entertainment. This was part of the show, and, in exchange for my shameless pleading, they offered a muttering of delighted approval just as JC slammed inside me.

I came instantly. I kept coming as he pounded into me without mercy, his thrusts fast and furious, refusing to let the rush of ecstasy subside until he was as wrung-out as I was.

He collapsed on top of me, then rolled us so we were face-to-face. Alternately, he studied me and kissed me, his fingers combing through my hair. "That was good, wasn't it? You loved it as much as I did, didn't you?"

"Yeah," I reassured him. "I really did." I glanced out the door at our onlookers, surprised I didn't feel awkward now that we'd finished. On the contrary, I felt quite comfortable, even when the curvy woman winked and her Latino friend gave me a thumbs-up. I might have blushed a bit, but I felt more giddy than embarrassed.

"I knew you did." He brought his thumb to run along my lower lip, and somehow I was positive he was already thinking about doing it again.

"I do have one concern," I said, nipping at the pad of his thumb.

His brows pressed together with worry. "What's that?"

"That this has the potential to become extremely addictive."

He brought his mouth down to mine, his chuckle getting lost in the depth of our kiss. I was glad he'd ended my ability to talk, because if he hadn't, I would have told him that I wasn't being completely honest.

I would have told him my concern was that I was pretty sure I was already addicted.

Chapter Eleven

Despite how hard it was to get a night away, going to The Open Door became a regular occurrence for us. We officially declared a regular date night and went to the party once a month through January. In February we went twice because Valentine's Day. In March we went twice because St. Patrick's Day and who doesn't want to public bang for that?

In April when I grew anxious because I couldn't find an excuse to go twice, I knew I had a problem.

"I think I'm obsessed." I plopped down into the booth at The Sky Launch where Alayna was working on plans for the club's redesign. She was finally back from her maternity leave, and I couldn't be happier because of course she was the only person I could talk to about my sex party addiction.

She looked up from the sketch she'd been studying. "You shouldn't use the word obsessed lightly around me."

With tendencies toward obsessive compulsive behavior, Alayna had a reason to be sensitive to the term.

Which was exactly why I'd come to her. "I'm not. I'm seriously concerned about it. I really think I have a problem."

"What problem?" Out of nowhere, my sister, Norma, sank down on the bench next to me. "Scoot over, will you?"

"Sure." I slid over to give her room, throwing a look across the table at Alayna that I hoped she understood meant to nix the conversation. Norma's arrival had been a complete surprise, and there was no way I was discussing this with her.

Typical Norma, she was all about prying. "What were you saying about having a problem?"

"Nothing," I said.

"Sex parties," Alayna said at the same time, obviously not getting the message I'd given her with my eyes.

Norma raised a brow as she reached for the lunch menu. "Sex parties? You're still doing that?"

"I'm not exactly comfortable talking about this with my sister." Sure, I'd told her about them in the beginning, when we were simply checking the club out, but now we'd officially become participants, and that was a whole different level of sharing.

Norma scowled. "Don't be silly. We both know I have sex."

Unfortunately, I *did* know. Walking in on her and her then boyfriend now husband Boyd while they were getting kinky was permanently seared in my brain. The most shocking part of it had been discovering that my overbearing, bossy, power-hungry sister was a bedroom submissive. It was a contradiction I had a hard time reconciling.

And I wasn't sure I wanted to try.

"I don't *want* to think about it," I told her. "I'd think you wouldn't want to think about *me* having sex either."

"We can talk about it without me thinking about it." She peered up from the menu she'd been scanning. "Can't you?"

I wasn't sure how to answer that. It wasn't like I *tried* to think about the quirky things she did with Boyd. Usually I didn't let my brain focus on the matter to get that far because I didn't like to even imagine my sister as a sexual being. She'd been too much like a mother to me, and that was just...gross.

But try telling her that.

"Why are you even here?" I asked in frustration.

"Had a meeting nearby and decided to stop by for lunch. It's good to see you too." She set down the menu and gave me a bright smile.

So she was staying. Okay, then.

I took a deep breath. This was all good. I hadn't seen Norma in awhile, and we'd always been close. It would be nice to chat with her. I could save the sex talk with Alayna for later.

"Why do you think you're a sex addict?"

I could feel my face turning bright red. "Alayna! Norma is still here."

"She just said she has no problem talking about it with you, and I'm dying to hear why you believe you're addicted. So spill some tea."

"Yeah, spill some tea," Norma echoed.

I cringed at my sister's attempt to be in on the current lingo as I propped my elbows on the table. I bent my neck and ran my fingers across my forehead. This topic wasn't going to go away, not now that Norma had gotten wind of it. She was unrelenting when she wanted to be, an admirable quality when I wasn't the one she was badgering. I'd learned over the course of a lifetime that resisting her attempts to pry was futile. Best just to dive in.

If I only focused on Alayna, maybe it wouldn't be too bad. "We've been going fairly regularly," I began, "As I've told you—"

Norma interrupted right off the bat. "You only told me you'd gone twice."

I swiveled in my seat so I could properly glare at her. "Look, I'm pretending you're not here right now, so help me out and refrain from commentary." Turning my attention back to Alayna, I went on. "We'd been going monthly, but then that wasn't enough so we started to go more often."

"What exactly is more often?" Alayna asked.

Before I could answer, Norma followed with her own questions. "Who's watching the kids when you go? The nanny?"

Irritated that she couldn't just sit silent and listen, my answer to Norma came out terse. "Sometimes the nanny. Mostly Ben." My brother and his husband were Jacob's favorite babysitters so I snagged him for overnights whenever he was available.

Then, to answer Alayna's inquiry... "We've kind of been going every other week."

"Why didn't you ever ask us to watch them? We love having the boys over." My sister was clearly offended.

I let out an exasperated huff. "You can watch them next time, okay? That's not the important part of this conversation, you know."

She held my glare for several seconds before holding her hands up in mock surrender. "I was just saying..." she mumbled under her breath.

Alayna, at least, could keep on topic. "Are the parties affecting your everyday life in any way?"

"We're banging like two horny teenagers, but neither of us are complaining about that."

"Nice." She reached across the table to give me a high-five. "If I wasn't so sleep deprived, I'd be jealous." She paused to consider. "No, I'm still jealous."

"Oh, please. You and Hudson are like rabbits. Even with twins."

"We are," she admitted with a smile. "Anyway, going to the parties isn't interfering with your responsibilities or your workload, right? You still manage the house and get the bills paid and your babies dressed and fed."

I frowned. "Yes? I mean, I do all that stuff as well as I ever have. I'm not exactly the Queen of Pentacles, but who is?"

Simultaneously, we both looked at Norma, who thankfully was too busy giving her order to a waitress to notice the unspoken compliment. My sister was the definition of the woman who could do it all. It would make me sick if I didn't admire her so much.

"This really doesn't sound like a problem," Alayna said with a shrug. "You just feel guilty because you've found something you love and enjoy that has nothing to do with your kids. It's hard for a lot of mothers to give themselves permission to take me time, but it's healthy if you do. Kudos to you. You could even go more. It meets once a week, right? Some couples have date nights that often. I don't know any of those couples, but I hear it's a thing."

"We have weekly date nights." With the waitress gone, Norma had tuned into the conversation again.

"Of course you do," I muttered.

Alayna's curiosity was piqued. "What kind of things do you do for your date nights?"

I propped my elbow on the table and leaned my cheek in my palm, preparing myself for whatever enviable response my totally on top of everything sister gave.

"We have season tickets to the opera and occasionally we'll see something on Broadway. Mostly, though, we go have kinky sex at Boyd's old apartment. We kept it just for that purpose when we got married."

I shifted my hand to my forehead, wishing I could unhear the words "kinky sex" come out of her mouth.

Alayna, however, saw it as validation. "See? Time out for sex is totally normal!" She turned back to Norma. "You really kept an apartment just for date night sex?"

"Please, don't encourage her, Laynie," I begged.

"We have a lot of toys we don't necessarily want around the kids," Norma said, as if I hadn't spoken. "I'm all about exposing children to early sex education, but there's a line. And some of our equipment is flat-out dangerous."

"Don't ask her about the toys!" I'd have to leave the table if she started talking about her private red room of pain.

"Can't be any worse than the toys you've told me about at your parties." Alayna had a point that I refused to acknowledge.

Norma turned to me with wide eyes. "Oh! Tell me about these toys."

"No!" I wasn't budging on this.

She paused a moment, her eyes narrowed. "The parties are good, then?" she asked, eventually.

"Yes," I said cautiously, wary of engaging with my sister on the topic. "They're all a little different, but, yes, they're all good."

"Huh." Her brow wrinkled in that way it always did when she had a new idea. "Maybe Boyd and I should get a membership. Can you invite us?"

"No. Way. I'd die. I cannot go if you're there." I couldn't be adamant enough.

"Why ever not? You told me you were just watching. We've been to strip clubs together. It can't be any different."

"You'd do more than just watch, and I can't be there for that." I wasn't ready to admit to her that JC and I were also doing more than just watching.

"Then we'll promise to just watch when you're there," she said, ever reasonable.

"What if we want to go every week?"

"Then we'll always just watch. Why are you being so weird about this?" Her expression changed as realization dawned. "Ohhh. You're doing more than just watching. I see."

"You are?" It was Alayna's eyes that were wide now.

"Don't judge me," I said to my friend. To my sister, I clarified. "We're not doing any of that domination/pain stuff that you do. Don't get any ideas that I'm into that."

"It sounds like *you're* judging *me*," she said.

"I'm not. I promise." I honestly didn't care what she did with Boyd, as long as she was happy, and she was. "I just want to be very clear about what isn't happening with me and JC."

She angled her body in my direction and gave me a stern stare. "The only way we'll be clear about what isn't happening with you and JC is if you'll tell us what *is*."

Alayna's expression demanded I answer as well.

Dammit, they'd ganged up on me.

"We're having *normal* sex, okay? Regular old normal sex." Quieter, I added, "While other people watch."

"Ohhhh," they said in unison, stretching the sound out as my confession sank in.

Alayna leaned back against the booth, her eyes wide with admiration. "That's not regular old normal sex if people are watching, Gwen. That's really hot, make-your-friends-jealous kind of sex."

"Sisters too," Norma said, equally impressed.

"It is really hot," I admitted. Really, really hot. And I loved it. So much that it worried me.

"How does that work? Are you on a stage or…?" Alayna trailed off, obviously trying to better imagine the situation.

"No, no, no. Definitely not on a stage." I didn't want her to think we were depraved. Or, at least, not that depraved. "We're in a bedroom most of the time and people watch from the hall. That's how it started, anyway. Then we started having sneaky sex in some of the shared rooms. You know, where no one knows you're doing it unless they're really paying attention. But soon we stopped being sneaky. And then we were being the opposite of sneaky, drawing attention to ourselves. But last week we actually played one of the kinky party games and later, when JC banged me reverse cowgirl style on a chaise lounge, I pulled down the bodice of my dress and so not only did everyone know we were getting it on, but they also saw my tits bouncing around while we did."

Oh, God. Maybe I *was* that depraved?

"People saw your tits? Oh dear. How will you ever recover?" Norma's sarcasm was annoying.

I ignored her and looked again to Laynie.

"If you're having a good time," she said, "I don't see what the problem is."

"The problem is that we had boundaries! And our boundaries are continually being crossed. And we're crossing them *at* the party, without talking about it beforehand, even though we keep swearing we won't, and it's all been good so far, but what happens when it isn't good anymore? What happens if we go too far?" We were doing things our way, but our way felt like it had gotten out of control.

The worst part was that being out of control was part of what I loved so much about the parties.

"What would be too far?" Alayna asked after a beat.

"I don't know." I did know. I'd thought a lot about it. "Like, if other people ended up getting involved. Maybe." As though it had just crossed my mind rather than being exactly the thing I was worried about.

"Make that a hard limit. Tell JC. He'll respect that." Norma used the lingo of someone who dealt with negotiating hard limits on a regular basis.

The problem was, my husband and I weren't in that lifestyle. We weren't as disciplined about our sex life as Norma and her husband were. "We keep saying no sharing and no touching other people, but what if we get carried away in the moment and ignore our rules?"

"You tell us," she countered. "If you did break your rules, what would happen?"

I had expected a speech about rules and why they had to be followed, so when she turned the question back on me instead, I was surprised and didn't have a quick answer.

When I was quiet for several seconds, she went on. "Sometimes these things are scary because they're new or because they're considered taboo, so you make rules so you won't have to deal with that fear. But often, these are also things you're truly interested in trying, and so, when you're in the moment and feeling less inhibited, the rules get ignored. Usually those are things you don't regret afterward because you secretly wanted it all along. Is that the case here? Are the lines you're worried about crossing actually lines you *want* to cross?"

I considered for a moment. The idea of a threesome was increasingly on my mind. JC continued to show interest in other women kissing and touching each other, and I couldn't forget the way he'd reacted when I'd kissed the girl at the kissing booth. I'd liked that, and while I wasn't exactly into doing more with another woman, I did like the idea of pleasing JC. I liked it a lot.

But if we did that, if we let someone else into our bed, what would happen to *us*?

Not sure I was ready to answer Norma's latest inquiry, I went back to the previous question—what would happen if we dropped the rules?

"I'm afraid I'll ruin my marriage," I said honestly. "I'm afraid that it would create jealousies and insecurities that we'd never get over. I'm afraid that by trying to make us into something better, we'll lose what we already have."

"That's valid," Alayna said. "And until you're okay with not knowing that answer, I'd be sure to keep those rules in place. They don't have to be forever, but for now."

Norma jumped in right on her heels, denying me a chance to respond. "You're talking about this with JC, right?"

I nodded, because we were talking. Maybe not about this specifically, but we talked.

"He doesn't want to ruin your marriage any more than you do," she continued. "If he knows what your limits are and how important it is to you to make sure you don't cross those limits then he's never going to let you cross them."

Alayna suddenly looked concerned. "He's not pressuring you into things you don't want to do, is he?"

"No. Definitely not. We never leave each other's sides at these things, and he always looks to me for consent. Just, what if I'm all into the consent and then later find out it was a bad decision?"

"You mean you want a crystal ball?" Norma asked. "Oh, well, if you'd just said that from the beginning."

I glared at her. "You aren't helping."

"Look, I understand why you're nervous," Alayna said. "Like your sister said, trying new things is always scary. That's why you're thinking about it so much. Because it's new and exciting and people tend to engage more with new and exciting things. You're not addicted. You're normal. The best part of this is that you're doing all of this with JC at your side instead of either of you sneaking around and exploring your desires on your own. Any mistakes you make will be together. And you guys are strong. You'll be able to steer back on course if need be. This is all good stuff."

"Not to mention that you're more relaxed than I've seen since before you had kids," Norma piped in.

"She definitely is," Alayna agreed.

"But…" I didn't know what I wanted to add after that but. They were right about all of it. I had to decide and commit to the limits we'd set until I was sure I wanted to abandon them. And then I had to trust that whatever happened, JC and I would be fine because we loved each other and our foundation was solid.

"No more buts," Alayna said, realizing what I needed to hear. "As your friend and sort of boss, I'm going to officially veto this as a concern and beg you to tell me more of the juicy stuff instead."

"I second the veto," Norma said, picking up a fry off the plate as the waitress set it down in front of her. "And the juicy stuff. Tell us all of that. Maybe I can pass some ideas on to Boyd."

"Don't say things like that to me!" I groaned.

"I won't tell you which stuff I pass on." She reconsidered. "Unless it turns out really good."

"Norma!" But I laughed. Really, what else could I do?

Chapter Twelve

I watched the bottle spin, my heart pounding as I wondered where it might stop. I held my breath as it spun. Would it land on me? On my husband? On someone else?

When it finally stilled, it pointed to a man so burly I was sure that two JCs could fit in his classic tuxedo. I let out the air I'd been holding and put my hands on my tummy where butterflies threatened to take flight. Any time it could be my turn, and that knowledge made me as excited as it made me anxious.

But mostly it made me anxious.

I wanted to play, that wasn't the problem. It was the first party we'd gone to since I'd talked to Alayna and my sister about my obsession with The Open Door, and, while I hadn't specifically decided I wanted to invite someone else into our fun, I had decided that I wanted to try engaging more.

The adult game of spin the bottle seemed like a perfect opportunity to do just that.

I exchanged a look at my husband as the burly man rolled the body dice and got the word ass. That was how this version of the game worked. One person would spin. Whoever it landed on would roll. The dice would then tell the spinner what part of the other person's body he or she should engage with—ear, neck, navel, mouth, nipples, or ass. Then an hourglass was flipped, the tiny sands that funneled through making sure that the activity lasted a full thirty seconds. And that it didn't go on past that.

It had seemed fairly innocent, not much different than the normal way the kissing game was played, but after four rounds, I was finding that The Open Door version could be quite risqué.

This was the first time anyone had gotten ass, and I was curious to see what the tattooed ginger who'd spun would do with the instruction. Ian—that was his name. I'd pretty much forgotten almost every one of the thirteen players' names from the intros, but his name had stuck for some reason. He seemed entirely too young to have as many tattoos as he did, way too young to be a guest at the party, but he stalked over to his prey like a pro, instructing the burly man to lie flat on his stomach. The hourglass was flipped, and Ian sat on his partner's back, facing his feet so he could grab two handfuls of the man's ass in his hands. Then he bent down and nipped both cheeks with his teeth before he ran his nose down the crack in between.

Even though both men were essentially still dressed, it was extremely erotic. Especially when Ian's nose followed the line of the crack between his partner's thighs. I was pretty sure he'd officially left the "ass" and encountered the "cock." The low groan that rumbled deep in the burly man's chest seemed to confirm my suspicions.

I swallowed, my cheeks going red. It was so naughty. I wasn't sure I could handle another man doing that to me if—when?—the bottle stopped on me. I was even less convinced my husband could handle it. Were we in over our heads?

A few minutes later, it appeared we were going to find out.

The last activity played out, the turn had moved on to the woman sitting next to Ian, a woman with beautiful dark skin, plump lips, and wide, exotic eyes. Her gaze met mine before the bottle had even stopped, as though she were psychic and knew where it was going to stop. Or maybe I was the person she wanted it to land on.

Either way, when the bottle finished its final rotation, it was pointing to me.

My shoulders relaxed with relief, glad that my partner was a woman. For JC's sake. Maybe for mine too. I was pretty sure I'd never be ready to have another man's hands, mouth, nose touch me in an erotic way. I was trying to be progressive, but, unless the guy was there to watch, I liked being a one-man kind of gal.

But a woman was a different story.

"Shoshanna," JC said quietly in that way that suggested he'd just remembered her name rather than that he was trying to inform me. I was grateful all the same since I had indeed forgotten. And if I was going to potentially have her nose in my ass—please, oh please not that—I wanted to know her name.

"This seems to be my lucky day," Shoshanna announced, and I felt the blush in my cheeks deepen.

As I always did in these situations, I glanced to JC, who smiled back at me, his eyes dark with interest.

I returned his smile. This had been the reason I'd wanted to play—to see that look on my husband's face. It was lighter fluid on the coals of my desire.

This was going to be good.

The butterflies had officially taken flight by the time I had the body dice in my hand. I blew on it and rolled it around in my hand, silently praying that I didn't get ass. I was so consumed with that possibility that I was completely unprepared for what showed up on the dice instead—nipple.

Oh, God. That was just as bad. Having my nipples played with by someone else, by a woman, for the first time, in front of other people? Yeah, that was possibly worse.

My entire body suddenly felt too hot, and now I was fairly certain the butterflies in my stomach were really flying razor blades.

I should bow out.

Except, as soon as the idea crossed my mind, I felt the heavy leaden weight of disappointment.

No, I wasn't bowing out. I wanted to do this. It was more than a little intimidating, but that's what made it so thrilling.

Shoshanna started crawling across the circle toward me, her brow lifted in an unspoken request for consent.

I nodded, hoping that was enthusiastic enough. Then, just to be clear I was on board, I asked, "So, tell me where you want me. Should I, uh, lie down?"

"You can stay right where you are, pretty lady," she said, a gorgeous yet wicked grin brightening her face.

Holy shit. That was...that was...

Surprisingly hot.

The quick peek at JC's face said he felt the same way.

The seconds stretched out in agony while I waited for Shoshanna to reach me. She took her time, building up the anticipation without wasting any grain of sand on the timer since it wasn't flipped until contact with the body part was made. My breaths became harder to get in and out, and I worried she could see the rapid fall of my chest. Worried she could see how nervous I was. How eager.

When she came to a stop in front of me, still on all fours, I couldn't take the wondering. "I'm breathing kind of hard. I guess I'm nervous," I said, outing myself.

"I noticed. I like it." She sank back on her legs into a kneeling position. With her eyes pinned on mine, she reached one long finger out toward my breast and swiped it in a circle, practically tracing the unseen edges of my areola. Immediately my nipple stiffened. Since I was braless, the peak was very evident through the thin satin of my gown.

"Nice," she said, as heat ran down my neck, disappearing into my cleavage.

"Flip the hourglass," someone nearby said, reminding the person assigned to the task to concentrate on his job.

"Timer started," he said a brief second later.

The interaction barely registered in my peripheral. My attention was elsewhere, on the teasing way Shoshanna plucked and pinched at my nipple, mixing bites of pain with soothing swipes of her fingertips. Arousal flooded me, making my thighs sticky and wet.

But it wasn't Shoshanna's hands that had me turned on—well, not *just* her hands. Throughout her tormenting caresses, my eyes were locked on JC's and what I saw on his face— his hooded lids, his dilated eyes, his unmasked expression of complete and utter lust—had electricity charging through my body like I'd been holding a lightning rod in a storm.

JC's excitement drove him to scoot closer, his gaze alternating from my face to my breast.

The movement drew Shoshanna's focus. "Want to help?" she cooed in his direction. "Her other nipple's feeling lonely, and I'm too consumed with this one to give it the attention it deserves."

Without hesitation, JC stretched his palm out to plump my other breast in the way that I liked best, a way that only he knew.

My breath caught audibly. The combination of his touch and hers sent a delicious shiver down my spine. My skin felt like fire underneath their fingers. I was burning with want. Burning for more. Burning to—

"Time!"

An involuntary groan escaped my lips as Shoshanna withdrew her hand. Self-conscious, I brought my hand to cover my mouth as if I could recall the sound. My cheeks were already too heated to form a proper blush, but my awkwardness was apparent to all.

"I liked it too, baby," she said with a wink.

JC brought his own hand to his lap, casually hiding the boner that I'd already noticed. Or bringing attention to it—either was possible. He looked from me to Shoshanna then back to me. He didn't have to say what he was thinking. I knew what he was thinking. I knew what he wanted.

And, suddenly, I was pretty sure I wanted it too.

Without saying a word, I stood up and stepped out of the circle, excusing myself from the game. JC followed suit. I took his hand and headed out of the room, feeling Shoshanna's intent stare chase after us.

I didn't turn back until I reached the doorway. With a nod, I beckoned her. I watched long enough to be sure she was coming, then, with a confidence I didn't know I possessed, I strutted from the room and led us to the bedrooms upstairs.

Chapter Thirteen

The night was still young, so finding an unoccupied bedroom wasn't difficult. I steered us toward the furthest one from the stairway. I stood aside to let JC and Shoshanna walk in past me, then shut the door behind them. Unlike the other times that my husband and I had taken to a room at an Open Door party, I didn't want anyone watching. This situation was plenty erotic on its own. Onlookers wouldn't make it hotter, they'd make it more awkward and nerve-wracking than it already promised to be.

With the door at my back, I looked at first JC then Shoshanna. They'd taken points on either side of the bed, both equidistant from me, unwittingly forming us into a triangle. The butterflies returned, flying so high that my entire torso was a flutter from my belly to the base of my throat.

Wow. We were really doing this.

I wiped a sweaty hand with the skirt of my dress and giggled, eliciting smiles from both my soon-to-be lovers. I cleared my throat and attempted to put myself together. "We're new at this," I explained to Shoshanna.

"I'm not," she said, reassuringly.

"Oh, good. You might need to take the lead."

She opened her mouth to say something along the lines of no problem, based on her confident expression, but before any words could be spoken, JC interjected. "Go to her, Gwen," he commanded.

Apparently he preferred taking the lead himself, newbie or not.

Or had he had a threesome before that I'd never bothered to ask about? I made a mental note to inquire about that. Later. At a more appropriate time.

Now, I had better things to think about than JC's past. Things like making my feet walk across the room. It was harder than it should have been with my knees knocking the way they were. Shoshanna's smile, though, was sexy and inviting, and that helped.

When I was only a couple of feet away, I paused to look to JC for the next instruction.

"Kiss her," he said, his voice rumbling deep in his chest. So low I felt it in my pussy. I felt it, and there was no way I could ignore the order. I took another step toward her. Then another.

A breath away, I suddenly got nervous. I'd kissed girls in high school playing spin the bottle and truth or dare and at the kissing booth, but I'd never kissed a girl with the intent to lead to more. It couldn't be much different than initiating a kiss with a man, but, before JC, I'd rarely taken the lead with men, either.

And it had been so long since I'd been with anyone besides my husband. I couldn't remember how first kisses were done.

Shoshanna, thankfully, was experienced and not at all shy. She closed the distance, bringing her mouth to mine. With firm pressure, she wrapped her lips around my bottom one. I tried to close my mouth for a proper kiss, but she pulled away slightly, taking my lip with her, teasing it, as though she were warming me up.

I eased back, not knowing what to do next.

I needn't have worried. She took care of that. After letting my lip go, she moved in again. This time she allowed me to participate in the kiss. Our mouths moved together awkwardly, our teeth clashing when we both turned the same direction at the same time. Once again, she paused. She raised her brows and I felt the silent demand that she be the one in control.

I nodded. The next time she moved in, I surrendered, following her lead, and soon our mouths moved together fluidly. The kiss built naturally from there, deepening when she licked into my mouth, urging my tongue to tangle with hers. Her palm came up to toy with my nipple, more assertively than she had during the game. My own arms felt weird dangling at my side, but I wasn't yet brave enough to fondle her breasts, so I brought them up to cradle her face. When I did, she let out a guttural moan that made my thighs tremble and my cunt leak.

Or, I thought she had.

Then I realized the sound had come from my husband.

With my mouth still attached to hers, I opened my eyes and peered in his direction. He had one knee on the bed, his hand stroking the straining bulge in his pants, his gaze glued to us.

Ah, fuck. That was sexy.

It was my turn to moan.

Without warning, Shoshanna turned us and pushed me back on the bed, her lips not leaving mine until I was breathless underneath her. Then her mouth traveled lower, to my chin, down my décolletage, down to my breast, where she sucked my nipple into her mouth through my dress.

My lips weren't alone for long. Seconds after she left, JC was bent over me, occupying them instead. He was more aggressive than she'd been, but his taste and movements were familiar, and my mouth danced easily with his. Though the angle of his face, upside-down over mine, blocked my view, I knew it was his hand that slipped under the bodice of my dress to plump my other breast. His touch was one I knew by heart. The contrast, though, between the well-acquainted caress of my husband and the thrillingly strange gropes of my new lover had me arching off the bed, begging for more, and when JC reached behind my neck to undo the lone button at the back of my dress, I nodded with enthusiastic consent.

With the back undone, it was easy to pull my arms out. JC peeled the bodice down to my waist and took one peaked nipple into his mouth, alternately sucking and teasing with his teeth. Shoshanna's approach was more torturous, licking around the tip before blowing a stream of hot air across the wet skin. Each technique alone could drive me crazy. Together, I was writhing as sparks of pleasure shot straight to my pussy.

It was like nothing I'd ever experienced, being adored by two people at once, all the attention focused on me. It felt selfish and glorious and I couldn't imagine how I'd lived my whole life without trying something so wildly wonderful before.

Wanting to give as well as take, I stretched up to stroke JC's cock. I could feel the heat of him through his dress pants, and, when I squeezed around his base like I knew he liked, he grew stiffer.

Feeling less inhibited now, I reached down for Shoshanna's breast, palming it tentatively before squeezing my hand around it. It was firmer than mine were these days, and I liked the feel of it in my hand. Loved it, even. Loved the contrast of her soft flesh compared to JC's stiff cock in my other hand. Loved exploring similar anatomy on a foreign landscape. I wanted more of this too, wanted her breast bare, wanted to explore her with my mouth.

But instead of granting me more access, she taunted me by giving me less, moving lower, kissing along my belly until she got to the area that was pulsing with need. I was still wearing my dress, otherwise my instinct would likely have been to tense up. With the material barrier, even as thin as it was, her attention was less of an invasion, and instead of pressing my thighs together, I spread them apart, giving her better access.

As she moved below my pubic bone, her kisses turned to nips and when she reached my engorged clit, she used her lips, opening and closing them over the sensitive bud with such expertise, an orgasm immediately began to build. Since I'd gone pantiless as well as braless, there wasn't much between her mouth and my pussy, and I could feel her, really feel her. Could feel her so intensely that I couldn't imagine how incredible she'd feel against me bare.

Soon, I hoped I wouldn't have to try to imagine.

Right now, though, this was more than enough. Unable to concentrate on stroking JC's cock any longer, I wove both my hands through Shoshanna's black hair, pulling on the corkscrew strands while JC returned to devour my mouth, continuing the assault on my nipple by rolling it between his thumb and forefinger.

The tension inside me curled and coiled, tightening, tightening, tightening at rapid speed, and then my climax was upon me, roaring through my body like the wind of a hurricane. With a strangled cry, I let myself get swept up in its magnitude, convulsing with the intensity of pleasure. Tears leaked from my eyes as lightning shot across my vision.

Still, JC and Shoshanna kept on, torturing me, tormenting me, not letting up until the orgasm had finished completely.

"That was so fucking hot," JC said between kisses.

"Incredibly hot," Shoshanna agreed, crawling back up my body.

JC pulled back, pressing his lips to the tip of my nose then each of my eyelids, letting Shoshanna reclaim my mouth. This time when I kissed her, I was unbridled. Even after the amazing orgasm, I was still filled with raw, primal lust that drove the frenzied movement of our mouths and tongues.

After several minutes of making out, I opened my eyes to look for JC and found him kneeling above my head, his jacket and shirt gone. He stared at us with fierce intensity, once again stroking the tent in his pants.

He needs attention. That *needs attention*, I thought.

Shoshanna must have had the same sort of idea, and, before I could do anything about it, she broke away from my mouth and stretched up until she was face-to-face with JC. After the briefest of hesitations, they simultaneously bent in for a searing kiss.

Below them, I watched. I could see everything from here, could see how their tongues twisted together as they explored each other's mouths. Could see the rapid rise and fall of Shoshanna's chest. Could see his fingers curl into her hair at the base of her neck, holding her in place.

It was potently sensual, and my body reacted to it, the steady pulse of need in my lower region increasing in speed and strength.

But my head...my head had a different reaction.

My head recognized the familiarity of his kiss, remembered times he'd kissed me that way. My head registered a blaring contradiction between what he was doing and all his promises that his kisses belonged to me, that he was mine—*only* mine—for all eternity.

I didn't like it.

I hated it.

As hot as the scenario seemed in theory, it was a totally different thing to actually watch my husband shower another woman with physical affection. As greedy and selfish as it likely made me, my jealousy was achingly real and palpable and unbearable, and when Shoshanna reached down to grab JC's cock—*my* husband's cock—I couldn't take it anymore.

I sat bolt upright, coming between her hand and his erection. "Stop!" I practically shouted.

Immediately they broke apart and two sets of eyes stared curiously at me.

Tears sprung to my eyes and my throat felt clogged. "I can't do this," I managed to say. Holding my dress over my breasts, I nudged Shoshanna until she moved a knee, and I could stand up.

Once on my feet, I turned toward them, my eyes cast down, unable to look directly at either of them. "I can't do this," I said again. "I thought I could, but I can't. I'm sorry. I'm so so sorry."

Before either of them could respond, I rushed into the ensuite, shutting and locking the door behind me. Then, I sank to the ground, wrapped my arms around my knees, and sobbed.

Chapter Fourteen

JC had always been good about giving me space when I needed it, but only for so long. He'd be knocking on the door sooner rather than later. So I only allowed myself a brief cry before I picked myself off my feet and tried to repair the damage the breakdown had done to my make-up.

About ten minutes later, I heard his gentle rap. "Gwen, baby?"

There was no question or request. Just my name and the endearment, and I was sure he was probably as confounded about what to do with me as I was.

I wasn't ready to talk about it, but I needed to get out of there.

Forcing the fakest smile I'd ever worn, I pushed the door open. The door to the hall was still closed, but JC was the only one in the room. I saw enough of him in my periphery to know he was once again fully clothed, which was good because it meant we could be gone quickly. What he was thinking or feeling was a mystery, however, since I refused to look at him directly.

"Can we go?" I asked, fussing unnecessarily with the buttons on the front of my dress.

"Of course. But, Gwen, should we talk?"

I'd started heading toward the door as soon as he'd said we could leave, so my back was to him when I said, "Not here."

My palm closed around the knob, but just as I started to open it, his hand landed flat on the oak of the door and pushed it closed. "Hold on a sec."

"JC, I said I don't want—" I jerked at the shock of his fingertips at the back of my neck. Immediately, I felt ashamed when I realized he was simply fastening the button in the back.

"Just wanted to make sure you were put together," he said softly. His fingers lingered, and the hot exhalation of his breath told me he was standing closer than I'd realized.

It took all my will not to melt into him. I felt like shit and wanted his comfort.

I also wasn't sure I deserved it.

So I steeled myself and stayed stick straight, my shoulders stiff. "Thanks," I mumbled, opening the door. Just. Had. To. Get. Out.

I walked at a clipped speed, my head down so as not to make accidental eye contact with anyone. I couldn't deal with human interaction. Even the innocent brush of a shoulder as I slipped past a body on the stairs made my stomach tighten. I didn't even want to imagine how I'd react if I bumped into Shoshanna.

God, I'd die of humiliation if I saw her.

The thought made me hurry even faster.

At the bottom of the stairs, JC caught up with me. I only knew because I felt his reassuring hand at the small of my back, a pressure I could recognize with my eyes closed.

"Go ahead and go. I'll take care of getting our things." He'd spoken too quietly for me to detect the underlying tone. The gesture was thoughtful, but maybe he was as embarrassed about my behavior as I was and wanted me out of sight.

Whichever it was, I was grateful. "I'll meet you in the lobby." Without waiting for his response, I pushed through the crowded foyer and escaped to the hallway. There were a few people out here as well, people who seemed to be coming instead of going. Luckily the elevator was only a few short yards away, and, when the doors closed, I was the only one inside.

Alone, I blew out a long stream of air and hugged myself around my waist. There was a lot I needed to think about, a whole hell of a lot to examine, but if I did it now, I'd fall apart. I concentrated on watching the numbers change as the floors passed.

Eighteen, seventeen, sixteen.

Did people know what happened?

Don't think about it. Twelve, eleven, ten, nine.

Was JC super mad at me? Did I just ruin my marriage?

A new sob caught in my throat.

One.

The doors opened, and I felt another rush of relief that there wasn't anyone in the lobby besides the doorman, who was too busy playing with his phone to notice me. But now I had to wait for my husband and I had no phone of my own, no numbers to watch change on a digital screen, and lots of buzzy buzzy noise in my head, begging for attention.

I paced, counting the steps it took to get to the other side of the lobby and back to the elevator. Twenty-seven to get to the outside doors. My stride quickened on the way back and it only took twenty-four. Back to the outside doors was twenty-five.

Just as I pivoted to make my return, the elevator doors opened, and there was JC, looking as sharp and handsome as ever, his expression tight, his hair a mess from...well, probably from someone running their fingers through it. Had it been him? Had it been me?

Fuck, had it been Shoshanna?

I was too wrapped up in the answer to remember to bow my head, and our eyes caught. His features softened ever so slightly, but his mouth stayed tight. Was that regret? Pity?

I didn't want to guess almost as much as I didn't want to know.

My gaze dropped to my feet and stayed there until he'd walked the twenty-seven/twenty-five steps to get to me, then I pushed through the glass door out into the spring night.

Except for when JC offered to give me his jacket, which I declined, we were quiet on the way home. The party had only been located three blocks away from our apartment, so we walked. The sounds of New York City traffic and the clip, clip, clip of my heels on the pavement made the silence feel less tense than if we'd been trapped together in a car, but it wasn't enough distraction to keep my head occupied.

What had Shoshanna said? She was surely angry. I'd left her with serious blue balls after she'd been so generous to me.

I was a terrible lover.

The Open Door would probably cancel our membership.

Had JC tried to give an explanation for me? What had *he* said to Shoshanna? Had their parting been awkward? Had he kissed her goodbye?

The knot in my stomach grew so tight I thought I might throw up.

God, what a mess I'd made.

Inside our apartment, I headed straight for our bedroom, wanting to be out of my clothes. Wanting to be out of my skin. JC followed on my heels, and before I could escape into my closet, he snagged my elbow, his grip firm and anchoring.

"Gwen, if you don't want to talk, can I say some things?"

I ignored the gentle tug inviting me into his arms. "Can I take a shower first? Please?"

He didn't answer, and he didn't let me go. I braved myself and lifted my eyes to find he was studying me with concern.

He wasn't mad at me. Or he wasn't as mad as he was worried. Of course he wouldn't be. He loved me. I knew that. I *knew* that.

It felt good to remind myself of that.

"We'll talk after," I said, my voice softer. "I promise." First, I had to figure out what I was going to say.

He nodded then, his lips twitching like he wanted to bend down and kiss my head but also wanted to respect my boundaries.

Respect won, and he let me go. "I'll be here if you need me," he said as I closed the bathroom door on him for the second time that night.

This time, I managed not to sink to the floor, despite my insides feeling like lead. Mechanically, I kicked off my shoes and stripped off my dress, leaving it in a pile where it fell on the marble floor, then I stepped into the walk-in shower, stood under the hot water, and let my brain try to unwind the tangle that I'd made.

The problem was that I hadn't made a firm decision to break our rule of no sharing before I'd broken it. Alayna had warned me about that.

The problem was that I was selfish and insecure and couldn't handle my husband touching another woman, no matter how certain I was of his love.

The problem was that I was too consumed with finding the ultimate erotic high when we'd been perfectly happy with what we'd already found.

The problem was that I'd talked to JC but not really. Not as much as I should have. Not specifically about what might happen if we invited someone else into our bed. Not about whether or not it was something we both wanted. I'd made the decision on my own, and that wasn't how we worked best. We worked best together.

Oh, yeah. That was it. That last one.

I shook my head at myself, wondering how I could possibly need to learn this lesson again so late in our relationship. It was something I'd thought we'd sorted out and had a firm handle on years ago, when JC had tried to make important decisions about what was best for us without my input and had almost forced me to announce to everyone at our wedding that he hadn't shown.

He *had* shown up in the end, with apologies and promises and so much love I couldn't stay mad for long. I'd reamed him thoroughly, though. And I'd made him vow to never think he could do better alone than we could together again.

He'd spent all the years since making it up to me, and I'd spent just as long reminding him about it, even though we'd long since passed being even.

Now, here I'd done the same exact thing.

Some adult I was.

Well, I could be an adult about it now. This was fixable, and afterward I'd be back in JC's arms where I belonged.

Suddenly, that was where I wanted to be more than anything.

I hurried through the act of washing my hair and scrubbing clean, and when I was out of the shower, a towel wrapped around me and another around my hair, I skipped my moisturizing routine and padded out to find my husband.

I didn't have to look far. He was in the bedroom, right where he'd said he'd be, in case I needed anything. He'd changed out of his suit and donned a pair of navy pajama bottoms and was now sitting on top of the bed covers, reading his iPad, the side table lamp the only light on.

He looked up at me as soon as I emerged from the bathroom, and as I started toward him, he set his tablet down, giving me all his attention.

When I reached him, I sank down on my knees on the floor beside him and took one of his hands in mine. "I'm sorry," I said.

"Oh, baby." He caressed my cheek with his thumb. "I don't need an apology. I need to know what's going on inside that head of yours."

"You don't even know what I'm sorry for."

He looked for a moment like he'd continue his reassurances of no apology necessary, but then, with a sigh, he said, "Fine. Tell me."

"I'm sorry for not telling you what's going on inside this head of mine."

He laughed, his dimples lighting up his entire face. Then he reached his hand out to pull me up on the bed with him. "Come here."

I came, curling into the crook of his arm where I fit so perfectly. "I wasn't sure I was into it," I said, not sure where to start so starting somewhere completely random. "I'd thought about the possibility a lot over the last few months. It had never been something I'd been particularly drawn to, but I really liked the way you reacted when I kissed that girl at the kissing booth."

"By it you mean a threesome?"

"Yeah, yeah. A threesome." The word seemed ridiculous when I said it out loud. Like, why the hell did I ever think I'd want that?

I shook my head. "I guess, in a way, I felt like I was the one getting at all of those parties, and you were the one giving. It was my kink to be watched. I pulled you into that without ever asking, and you'd been so generous to go along."

"Uh, you think I was just going along because I'm nice?"

I put my hand up to silence him. "Okay, I knew you liked it too, but let me finish. It was still *my* kink, and as I started studying your reactions to me kissing another woman and the idea of girl-on-girl, I realized that must be your kink. And I wanted to give you your kink more than I wanted to figure out whether or not it was something I was really okay with going along with. Obviously, I wasn't in the end. When I watched the two of you kissing…" My stomach curled, remembering. I shook the image off. "The idea seemed hot, but the actual doing was…not the same. I'm sorry for that too. For starting something I couldn't finish, and for not being able to meet your needs the way you met mine, but mostly for not talking to you about any of this to begin with."

"Gwen?" He brought my chin up to meet his gaze with two fingers, sending the towel that was precariously piled on my head off balance. Wet strands of hair fell down around my face as I gave him my complete attention. "Are you listening to me right now? Because I need you to really be listening."

"Yes. I'm listening." My heart tripped in anticipation of whatever Very Important Thing he was about to tell me.

"I don't care about having a threesome. That's not my kink. My kink isn't girl-on-girl, either, though I don't think there's a straight man alive who doesn't think that's fucking hot, so any hard-ons I get from that are just the nature of me being a guy. You want to know what my kink is?"

"What?"

"My kink is *you*." He let that sink in before going on. "My kink is whatever turns you on. Whatever gives you pleasure. My kink is being there when your eyes go hazy and your breath stutters and your toes curl and your cheeks pink. Whatever it is that brings that to you, I'm into it."

"Really?" I blinked back tears.

"Yes, *really*." He thought for a second. "I mean, I'd prefer not to test how far I could go with that because I don't think I could whip you or hit you or ride you like a horse, and I definitely couldn't stand another man touching you, which probably makes me a selfish pig, but that's who I am. You're mine, and I'm not sharing."

"That was exactly how I felt about you kissing Shoshanna. I wanted to be turned on by seeing you get some, but all I could think was, he's mine, bitch. Hands off."

He chuckled. As his smile faded, he traced the line of my jaw. "Actually, that's kind of hot. I like being yours. I like being *only* yours."

"Me too." I turned my face to catch his finger between my lips and sucked on it, watching as his eyes grew dark. "Although…" I let his finger fall from my mouth.

"Yes?"

"It was really hot when you both played with my nipples at once." My pussy clenched at the memory.

"Fuck, that was wicked hot." He nearly growled.

"And I loved being kissed by you while she did that crazy stuff to my clit."

"I almost came in my pants when you did. You were so beautiful."

"I tried to imagine what it would feel like if she was going down on me without my dress in the way. And with your cock in my mouth instead of your tongue."

His hand returned to my cheek, this time caressing it with his knuckles. "Is that what you want, baby? Is that what would bring you pleasure? We could have a rule that the only person I touch is you."

"No," I said, shaking my head for emphasis. "It was fun, but I don't want to do that again. I like being watched, but I don't want to involve anyone else again, if that's all right."

"Totally all right."

"But that doesn't mean we can't fantasize about it."

His smile crept slowly over his lips. "In that case, you stroke my cock instead of suck it. So I can watch her head moving between your thighs *and* see you come."

"Oh, of course. A much better scenario."

His hand worked the towel around my torso loose. We both knew where this was going, and I wasn't going to protest in the least.

"Or," I said, "You sit like you are now." Naked, I nudged his legs apart so I could kneel between them. Bending over, I nipped softly at his erection through his pjs but left my butt up in the air behind me. "And she's going down on me from behind."

He reached a long arm around to play with my pussy from that direction. "Like this?"

"Mm hm." I worked his pants down far enough to expose his beautiful cock.

"Is this her tongue playing with your clit?" He used the pad of his finger to tickle the sensitive bud.

"Mm hm." This time his cock was in my mouth and the sound reverberated around it, causing it to thicken. God, that made me wet.

"Now her tongue is rimming your pussy." He traced my hole. "You love it when she sticks it inside too, don't you?"

I didn't say anything coherent after that. JC continued to describe naughty images for a while, but his phrases grew shorter until they were just dirty words. Then there were the I love you's, murmured reverently in my ear. Tomorrow there would be noise and chaos and melt-downs and baby giggles, but tonight there was this. The kinds of words that reminded us where we started and how it was that we came to get all those other wonderful noises in our lives.

And then there were no words at all, just moans and gasps and the sounds of bodily fluids gushing and skin slapping against skin. All those sorts of sounds that accompanied really good sex.

The sorts of sounds we made best together.

* * * *

Also from Laurelin Paige and 1001 Dark Nights, discover Dirty Filthy Fix and Falling Under You.

Sign up for the 1001 Dark Nights Newsletter
and be entered to win a Tiffany Key necklace.

There's a contest every month!

Go to www.1001DarkNights.com to subscribe.

**As a bonus, all subscribers can download
FIVE FREE exclusive books!**

Discover 1001 Dark Nights Collection Six

Go to www.1001DarkNights.com for more information.

DRAGON CLAIMED by Donna Grant
A Dark Kings Novella

ASHES TO INK by Carrie Ann Ryan
A Montgomery Ink: Colorado Springs Novella

ENSNARED by Elisabeth Naughton
An Eternal Guardians Novella

EVERMORE by Corinne Michaels
A Salvation Series Novella

VENGEANCE by Rebecca Zanetti
A Dark Protectors/Rebels Novella

ELI'S TRIUMPH by Joanna Wylde
A Reapers MC Novella

CIPHER by Larissa Ione
A Demonica Underworld Novella

RESCUING MACIE by Susan Stoker
A Delta Force Heroes Novella

ENCHANTED by Lexi Blake
A Masters and Mercenaries Novella

TAKE THE BRIDE by Carly Phillips
A Knight Brothers Novella

INDULGE ME by J. Kenner
A Stark Ever After Novella

THE KING by Jennifer L. Armentrout
A Wicked Novella

QUIET MAN by Kristen Ashley
A Dream Man Novella

ABANDON by Rachel Van Dyken
A Seaside Pictures Novella

THE OPEN DOOR by Laurelin Paige
A Found Duet Novella

CLOSER by Kylie Scott
A Stage Dive Novella

SOMETHING JUST LIKE THIS by Jennifer Probst
A Stay Novella

BLOOD NIGHT by Heather Graham
A Krewe of Hunters Novella

TWIST OF FATE by Jill Shalvis
A Heartbreaker Bay Novella

MORE THAN PLEASURE YOU by Shayla Black
A More Than Words Novella

WONDER WITH ME by Kristen Proby
A With Me In Seattle Novella

THE DARKEST ASSASSIN by Gena Showalter
A Lords of the Underworld Novella

Also from 1001 Dark Nights:
DAMIEN by J. Kenner

Discover More Laurelin Paige

Dirty Filthy Fix: A Fixed Trilogy Novella

I like sex. Kinky sex. The kinkier the better.

Every day, it's all I think about as I serve coffee and hand out business agendas to men who have no idea I'm not the prim, proper girl they think I am.

With a day job as the secretary to one of New York's most powerful men, Hudson Pierce, I have to keep my double life quiet. As long as I do, it's not a problem.

Enter: Nathan Sinclair. Tall, dark and handsome doesn't come close to describing how hot he is. And that's with his clothes on. But after a dirty, filthy rendezvous, I accept that if we ever see each other again, he'll walk right by my desk on his way to see my boss without recognizing me.

Only, that's not what happens. Not the first time I see him after the party. Or the next time. Or the time after that. And as much as I try to stop it, my two worlds are crashing into each other, putting my job and my reputation at risk.

And all I can think about is Nathan Sinclair.

All I can think about is getting just one more dirty, filthy fix.

* * * *

Falling Under You: A Fixed Trilogy Novella

Norma Anders has always prided herself on her intelligence and determination. She climbed out of poverty, put herself through school and is now a chief financial advisor at Pierce Industries. She's certainly a woman who won't be topped. Not in business anyway.

But she's pretty sure she'd like to be topped in the bedroom.

Unfortunately most men see independence and ambition in a woman and they run. Even her dominant boss, Hudson Pierce has turned down her advances, leaving her to fear that she will never find the lover she's longing for.

Then the most unlikely candidate steps up. Boyd, her much-too-young and oh-so-hot assistant surprises her one night with bold suggestions and an authoritative demeanor he's never shown her in the office.

It's a bad idea…such a *deliciously bad* idea…but when Boyd takes the reins and leads her to sensual bliss she's never known, the headstrong Norma can't help but fall under his command.

Slay One: Rivalry

Slay Quartet Book 1
By Laurelin Paige
Now Available

Edward Fasbender is a devil.

He's my father's business rival, a powerful, vicious man who takes what he wants and bows to no one. I only took the meeting because I was curious. I thought he was going to offer me a job.

But that's not what he's after at all. His proposal is much more intriguing, and I see an opportunity. An opportunity to turn the tables and bring down the devil.

I've gotten in trouble playing these games before. I know when the risk is too great, when the stakes are too high. I know how to be cold and strong-willed and destructive. I know how to withstand dominant men with arrogant charm and rugged features.

Yet I can't resist taking on Edward.

And I can't resist the pull he has on me.

Soon I'm not so sure which side of the battle I'm standing on--if I'm the warrior meant to slay,

Or the one who will be slain.

Slay is Book One of Four in _New York Times, Wall Street Journal_, and _USA Today_ bestselling author Laurelin Paige's next dark and edgy series.

* * * *

"You really screwed this one up, Celia. Hudson is officially out of reach. You let him slip away, and now everything you dreamed of is over."

I rolled my eyes, even though my mother couldn't see my face through the phone. I was tired of this speech. I'd heard a variation of it at least three times a week since my childhood friend had gotten married over two years ago.

As for my dreams being over...well, it had been a long time since I'd imagined myself ending up with Hudson Pierce. That was my mother's aspiration, not mine. Not anymore.

There wasn't any use in arguing with her. She found some sort of comfort in lamenting over her daughter's failures, and this particular lament was one of her favorites.

"From what Sophia says, he's even more devoted now to this marriage than he ever was, and I'm not at all surprised. A man will leave a wife easily enough, but when she gets pregnant, forget it. He's sticking around."

I leaned my head against the window of my Lyft car and sighed. "How is Sophia these days?" It was a manipulative redirection on my part. It disgusted me that she pretended otherwise, but Hudson's mother wasn't exactly on friendly terms with Madge Werner like she once was.

Pity.

That was also my fault. Hudson's fault too, not that either of our mothers would ever concede that fact.

I knew my tactic worked when my mother huffed loudly in my ear.

Just as I'd thought. My mother hadn't directly spoken to Hudson's mother about any of this. Likely, she'd picked it up through the grapevine. A friend of a friend or overheard it at a charity luncheon. What else did the rich bitches do these days to keep themselves entertained?

My own methods of amusement certainly weren't of the popular variety. But they were definitely more fun.

Or they once were, anyway. Even The Game had lost its spark in recent years.

"I don't even know why I bother talking to you about this," my mother droned on. "It's your own fault you're not with Hudson."

There was his name again. *Hudson.* There had been a time when it hurt to hear it. A time when immense agony had wracked through my body at the two simple syllables. That was a lifetime ago now. The bruise he'd left was permanent and yellowed with age, and I pressed at it sometimes, saying his name, recalling everything that had transpired between us, just to see if I could provoke any of those emotions again.

Every time I came up empty.

I owed that to him, I supposed. He'd been the one to teach me The Game. He'd been the one to teach me how to feel nothing. How to *be* nothing. How ironic that his life today was happy and complete and *full*.

Good for you, Hudson. Good for fucking you.

My mother was still yammering when the car pulled up at my destination. "You don't even realize how much you gave up when you let him get away, do you? Don't expect to do better than him. We both know you can't."

Indignation pierced through my hollow cocoon; anger in its varied forms was the one emotion that seemed to slip in now and again. My mother didn't know shit about me, no matter how close she perceived our relationship. Couldn't *do better* than Hudson? God, how I longed to prove her wrong.

But I didn't have any ammunition. I had nothing. I wasn't dating anyone, not really. I had my own interior design company that barely made enough to pay expenses, and I didn't even take a salary for myself. I was a trust fund baby for all intents and purposes, living off my father's business, Werner Media. And while all of my choices were purposeful, I couldn't exactly explain to my mother that the majority of my time and energy was spent on playing The Game. There was no one who would understand that, not even Hudson anymore.

With no comeback, my best bet was to end the call.

"I'm at my meeting. I have to go now, Mom." My tone was clipped, and I brusquely hung up before she could respond.

I gave my driver a digital tip, threw my cell phone in my bag then climbed out of the car. It was hot for early June. Humidity hung like thick cologne, and it clung to me even after I entered the lobby of the St. Regis Hotel. I was running late, but I knew this building from a lifetime of living among the upper crust of New York, and I didn't have to stop to ask for directions. The meeting rooms were a quick elevator ride up one floor to the level that had originally been John Jacob Astor's living quarters. The hotel had been kept in the elegant chic design of his time, and, while pompous in its style, I found the luxurious decor both timeless and elegant.

Since I was in too much of a hurry to admire the scenery, I headed straight to my destination. Inside the foyer for the Fontainebleau Room, I paused. The doors were shut. Was I supposed to knock or walk right in?

I was already digging out my phone to text my assistant, Renee, when I noticed a man in a business suit sitting behind a small table at the opposite end of the foyer. He seemed to be deeply focused on the book he was reading and hadn't yet seen me. I didn't know what the man I was meeting with looked like so I couldn't say if this was him or not.

Cursing myself for not being more prepared, I approached him. "Excuse me, I'm Celia Werner, and I'm supposed to—"

The man barely looked up from his reading when he cut me off. "I'll let him know you're here. Have a seat." He propped his book open by placing it face down on the table and then stood and circled around it to the door of the Fontainebleau. He knocked once then opened it, disappearing inside.

Somewhat baffled at the curt greeting, I scanned the foyer and found a bench to sit on. I took out my phone and shot a text to Renee.

Why isn't this guy meeting me at the office again?

I rarely took initial client meetings anywhere else. When Renee had first told me about the appointment, I'd assumed I was being hired by a committee or a board of directors and that they'd requested to interview me as part of a general meeting of some sort. It made sense in that case to go to them rather than the other way around. But something about the vibe of the situation made me start to doubt my first assessment. If there was an entire committee behind the closed doors, why had the man who greeted me said "him"? And wouldn't I have heard voices or people noises when the door had briefly been open?

While I waited for Renee's response, I pulled the client file from my bag and looked over the papers inside. The usual client questionnaire was on top, but, unlike usual, it was completely blank. I flipped to the next page, a background report. I ordered these on any client I considered taking on, not so much as a safety precaution, but more out of flagrant curiosity. My best games had been inspired by skeletons of the past, and I never passed up an opportunity to play.

I had no intention of taking on this particular client, however. In fact, I was only meeting with him so I could turn him down. The reason was laid out in bold in the first line of his information sheet: *Edward M. Fasbender, Owner and CEO of Accelecom*.

I didn't know much about Accelecom and even less about Edward Fasbender, but what I did know was that the hardball strategies of his London-based company were the primary reason Werner Media had never been able to penetrate the UK market. My father would be livid if I ever worked for his competitor, but he might be delighted to hear me tell him I'd rejected their offer. Proud, even.

At least, I hoped he would be. God only knew why I cared so deeply to please the man, but I did. It was ingrained in me at an early age to cater to the men who held dominion over me. My father was the lord of our household. If I could make him happy, I was sure my mother would stop her eternal lamenting. If I could make him happy, maybe I could *be* happy.

It was a ridiculous notion, but it had deep roots inside me.

I scanned through the rest of the report on Fasbender. Married very young. Divorced for several years. Hadn't remarried. Two nearly grown children. His father had also owned a media company that had been sold when Edward was a teen, just before both his parents had died. He'd built Accelecom from practically nothing, turning it into a multibillion-dollar company before he'd even turned forty-two, which would be in September. It was all pretty standard information, but, with years of experience, it was enough to help me create a solid picture of what kind of man Edward M. Fasbender was. Driven, calculating, strategic, monomaniacal. His dating history was too sparse for him to be attractive. He likely had to pay for his sex and didn't mind doing so. Egocentric and misogynistic probably as well, if I knew this kind of man, and I did. It would be fun rejecting his offer of employment, as shallow as the move might be.

My cell buzzed.

RENEE: **He insisted on meeting at the hotel. You approved that before. Is that still okay?**

I'd been eager to be amenable, I remembered now. The more congenial I was in the outset, the more surprising the rejection.

It's fine. Did he say what the project was going to be?

Something office related, I suspected, since there was a committee involved. Oh, that was going to be even more fun, turning him down in front of people.

RENEE: **He said he'd only discuss it in person.**

I added *controlling* to the list of character traits. And he definitely had a small dick. There was no way this asshole was packing.

Before I could ask Renee anything else, the door to the meeting room opened and the man from before stepped out. "He's ready for you now," he said, again making it sound like Mr. Fasbender was alone.

I shut the file folder, but didn't put it back in my bag, too eager and intrigued to bother with the hassle. I stood up and walked to the door of the Fontainebleau. As soon as I crossed over the threshold, I paused and frowned. Every time I'd been here in the past, the room had been set up with several round tables, banquet style. This time there was only one long boardroom type table, and though there were several chairs lined up around it, no one was sitting at them. My gaze swept the space and knocked into the one other person in the room—a man who appeared to be the same age the report had given for Fasbender.

But if this really was Edward Fasbender, I had grossly fucked up on my assessment of him. Because this man was not just attractive, he was overwhelmingly so. He was tall, just over six feet by my guesstimation. His expensive midnight-blue tailored suit showcased his svelte build, and from the way his jacket sleeves hugged his arms, it was obvious he worked out. He was fair-skinned, as his German name suggested, but his hair was dark and long at the top. While it had been tamed and sculpted in place, I imagined it floppy in its natural state. His brows were thick, but flat and expressionless, his eyes deep-set and piercing, lighter than my own baby blues, though maybe it was his periwinkle tie that brought them out so vibrantly. Whatever the reason, they were mesmeric. They made my knees feel weak. They made me catch my breath.

And his face!

His face was long with prominent cheekbones, his features rugged without being worn. He was clean shaven at the moment, but I was sure he could pull off scruff without looking gritty if he tried. His lips were full and plump with a well-defined v at the top. Two faint creases ran between his eyebrows making him appear intensely focused, and the slight lines that bookended his mouth gave him a permanent smirk, even when his mouth was just at rest.

Though, he might have meant the smirk in the moment. Considering the way I was standing frozen gawking at him, it was highly likely.

I shook my head out of my stupid daze, put on an overly bright smile, and started toward him, my hand outstretched. "Hi, I'm Celia Wern—" Before I could finish my introduction, the heel of my shoe caught on the carpet, and I tripped, spilling the contents of his file all over the floor.

Blood rushed up my neck and into my face as I crouched down to pick up the mess. It was awkward kneeling down in my pencil skirt, but

I was more concerned about gathering the papers before he saw them. It only took five seconds before I realized the concern was unnecessary, because, even though I'd dropped the pages at his feet, he was not bending down to help me. I was right about his character, it seemed. Arrogant, egocentric. Asshole.

I shoved the papers back in the file and shot a glare up at him, which turned out to be a mistake, because there he was, peering down at me with that perma-smirk, and something about the position I was in and his exuding dominance sent a shiver through my body. My skin felt like it was on fire, and goosebumps paraded down my arms. His presence was overpowering. Overwhelming. Unsettling.

My mouth dropped open in surprise. Men didn't make me feel this way. *I* made men feel this way. *I* overpowered the men around me. *I* overwhelmed them. *I* unsettled them.

I didn't like it. And yet, I also kind of did. It wasn't only an unusual feeling, but it was a *feeling*. It had been a long time since I'd felt anything, let alone something so startling.

I swallowed and prepared to rise when he surprised me again, finally stooping down to my level.

"Edward Fasbender," he said, holding out his hand.

With a scowl, I took it. My hand felt warm in his tight grip, and I let him hold on past the length of a standard handshake, let him help lift me back to a standing position before I withdrew it sharply.

He smirked at this too—that mouth smirked at everything, but I could feel the smirk in his eyes as well. "I've been looking forward to meeting you, Celia," he said in his distinguished British dialect. "Have a seat, will you?"

If there had been any logic to not taking a seat, I would have continued to stand, simply because I hated conceding any more control to him than I already felt I had. But there wasn't anything practical about standing, so I threw my bag and the file on the table, pulled out a chair and angled it toward the head where, if the laptop and phone sitting there were any indication, I surmised he was going to sit.

"I hadn't realized I'd only be meeting with you, Mr. Fasbender." I purposefully didn't scoot the chair back into the table so he could have a prime view while I crossed one long leg over the other. I had nice legs. They were two of my best weapons.

The bastard didn't even glance down. With his eyes pinned on mine, he unbuttoned his jacket and sat in the seat I'd assumed he'd take.

"Edward, please," he said sternly. He'd already made it clear he meant to call me Celia, even without my invitation to do so.

"As I was saying, *Edward*, I would have insisted we met in my office if I'd known you were reserving a meeting room simply for my benefit."

He tilted his head, his stone expression showing nothing. "It wasn't simply for your benefit. I've been using this room as my office while I'm in the States meeting with potential investors. It's unconventional, perhaps, but I'm already staying in the hotel, and so the location has proved convenient. Plus, I rather like the setting, don't you?"

I ignored how much I liked the low timbre of his voice and surveyed my surroundings once more. The Fontainebleau was one of the more lavish meeting rooms in the hotel. With the numerous crystal chandeliers, gold leaf plating, and ornate molding, the decor seemed to have been directly inspired by Versailles. I appreciated the luxurious look, but this was a bit on the abundant side, particularly when being used as an office. The fact that he liked it said more about his character. I added pompous and extravagant to my earlier assessment. He was probably even going to use the room as an example of whatever it was he wanted me to design for him.

No. Just no. Even if I were accepting his job offer, which I wasn't.

Refraining from commenting on the decor, I turned back to my subtle admonishment. "I'm sure this is convenient for you, but our discussion will be limited because of it. I've brought my computer and a portfolio, which will show you some of my work, but this would be much easier if you could see the models in my office. Maybe we can reschedule and meet there at a later time?" It would be even more delightful to reject him after stringing him along.

"That won't be necessary. I'm not interested in your design work."

The hairs on the back of my neck pricked up in warning, and I was suddenly glad for the man outside the door. Not that I couldn't handle myself. I'd been in much more precarious situations than this and survived.

"I'm sorry," I said, my voice cool and steady from practice. "I don't believe I understand." Though, I was beginning to have my suspicions. If I wasn't here about a design project, this meeting could only have to do with my father.

"Of course you don't. I didn't have any intention for you to understand until I was ready to explain."

He was such an arrogant piece of work. If I wasn't completely aroused with curiosity, I would have been out the door at this point.

"Since I'm here now, I'd appreciate it if you'd go ahead and fill me in. What is it you want from me?"

He leaned back in his seat, somehow seeming just as upright with his posture even in the reclined position. "What I want, Celia, is quite simple—I want you to marry me."

About Laurelin Paige

With millions of books sold, Laurelin Paige is the *NY Times*, *Wall Street Journal*, and *USA Today* Bestselling Author of the Fixed Trilogy. She's a sucker for a good romance and gets giddy anytime there's kissing, much to the embarrassment of her three daughters. Her husband doesn't seem to complain, however. When she isn't reading or writing sexy stories, she's probably singing, watching *Killing Eve* and the *Walking Dead*, or dreaming of Michael Fassbender. She's also a proud member of Mensa International though she doesn't do anything with the organization except use it as material for her bio.

You can connect with Laurelin on Facebook at www.facebook.com/LaurelinPaige or on twitter @laurelinpaige. You can also visit her website, www.laurelinpaige.com, to sign up for e-mails about new releases.

Discover 1001 Dark Nights

Go to www.1001DarkNights.com to subscribe.

COLLECTION ONE
FOREVER WICKED by Shayla Black
CRIMSON TWILIGHT by Heather Graham
CAPTURED IN SURRENDER by Liliana Hart
SILENT BITE: A SCANGUARDS WEDDING by Tina Folsom
DUNGEON GAMES by Lexi Blake
AZAGOTH by Larissa Ione
NEED YOU NOW by Lisa Renee Jones
SHOW ME, BABY by Cherise Sinclair
ROPED IN by Lorelei James
TEMPTED BY MIDNIGHT by Lara Adrian
THE FLAME by Christopher Rice
CARESS OF DARKNESS by Julie Kenner

COLLECTION TWO
WICKED WOLF by Carrie Ann Ryan
WHEN IRISH EYES ARE HAUNTING by Heather Graham
EASY WITH YOU by Kristen Proby
MASTER OF FREEDOM by Cherise Sinclair
CARESS OF PLEASURE by Julie Kenner
ADORED by Lexi Blake
HADES by Larissa Ione
RAVAGED by Elisabeth Naughton
DREAM OF YOU by Jennifer L. Armentrout
STRIPPED DOWN by Lorelei James
RAGE/KILLIAN by Alexandra Ivy/Laura Wright
DRAGON KING by Donna Grant
PURE WICKED by Shayla Black
HARD AS STEEL by Laura Kaye
STROKE OF MIDNIGHT by Lara Adrian
ALL HALLOWS EVE by Heather Graham
KISS THE FLAME by Christopher Rice
DARING HER LOVE by Melissa Foster
TEASED by Rebecca Zanetti
THE PROMISE OF SURRENDER by Liliana Hart

HALLOW BE THE HAUNT by Heather Graham
DIRTY FILTHY FIX by Laurelin Paige
THE BED MATE by Kendall Ryan
NIGHT GAMES by CD Reiss
NO RESERVATIONS by Kristen Proby
DAWN OF SURRENDER by Liliana Hart

COLLECTION FIVE
BLAZE ERUPTING by Rebecca Zanetti
ROUGH RIDE by Kristen Ashley
HAWKYN by Larissa Ione
RIDE DIRTY by Laura Kaye
ROME'S CHANCE by Joanna Wylde
THE MARRIAGE ARRANGEMENT by Jennifer Probst
SURRENDER by Elisabeth Naughton
INKED NIGHTS by Carrie Ann Ryan
ENVY by Rachel Van Dyken
PROTECTED by Lexi Blake
THE PRINCE by Jennifer L. Armentrout
PLEASE ME by J. Kenner
WOUND TIGHT by Lorelei James
STRONG by Kylie Scott
DRAGON NIGHT by Donna Grant
TEMPTING BROOKE by Kristen Proby
HAUNTED BE THE HOLIDAYS by Heather Graham
CONTROL by K. Bromberg
HUNKY HEARTBREAKER by Kendall Ryan
THE DARKEST CAPTIVE by Gena Showalter

Also from 1001 Dark Nights:

TAME ME by J. Kenner
THE SURRENDER GATE By Christopher Rice
SERVICING THE TARGET By Cherise Sinclair
TEMPT ME by J. Kenner

On behalf of 1001 Dark Nights,

Liz Berry and M.J. Rose would like to thank ~

Steve Berry
Doug Scofield
Kim Guidroz
Jillian Stein
InkSlinger PR
Dan Slater
Asha Hossain
Chris Graham
Kasi Alexander
Jessica Johns
Dylan Stockton
Richard Blake
and Simon Lipskar

Made in the USA
Middletown, DE
08 September 2019